"King's smoothly executed and addictive series returns, offering cinematic action and a high body count."—*Kirkus Reviews*

How could a little murder-for-hire scam go so wrong?

The Travelers and a computer hacker are operating a dark web con, taking cash from suckers who think they're hiring contract killers. Easy money. And no one to complain to the police. But when an actual killer comes after them, they're on the hunt for payback.

Who sent the assassin who killed their partner? And why is he stalking a newspaper reporter?

Once the Travelers figure out who they're up against, they set a plan in motion to rob him and take revenge, but as the cat-and-mouse game progresses, and the police get involved, the Travelers find they're moving through a quagmire of drugs, sex trafficking, and greed where any misstep could lead to the morgue.

The Dark Web Scam is a hard-charging crime thriller. If you like criminal machinations, fast-paced action, and devious plot twists, you'll love the ninth novel in the Travelers series.

The Travelers

The Double Cross: A Travelers Prequel
The Traveling Man: Book One
The Computer Heist: Book Two
The Blackmail Photos: Book Three
The Freeport Robbery: Book Four
The Kidnap Victim: Book Five
The Murder Run: Book Six
The Casino Switcheroo: Book Seven
Thicker Than Thieves: Book Eight
The Dark Web Scam: Book Nine

THE DARK WEB SCAM

THE TRAVELERS: BOOK NINE

MICHAEL P. KING

BLURRED LINES PRESS

Blurred Lines Press

The Dark Web Scam

Michael P. King

ISBN 978-1-952711-02-2

Cover design by Paramita Bhattacharjee at creativeparamita.com

The Dark Web Scam is a work of fiction. The names, characters, places, and events are products of the author's imagination or are used fictitiously. Any similarity to real persons or places is entirely coincidental.

Always for Sarah

1

THE SCAM

The Traveling Man and his wife, now going by the names Philip and Carrie Benson, sat on either side of Merlin Jimenez, reading the screen of a desktop computer that was set up on a folding table. Philip, a little over fifty, was sporting a salt-and-pepper goatee. He had the hard body of a retired athlete and a face you wouldn't pick out in a police lineup. Carrie, auburn hair cascading around her shoulders, was in her early forties but passed for late thirties. People often thought they remembered her from a popular romance movie they just couldn't quite place. The house, an empty two-bedroom stucco in a Denver suburb, was in a quiet neighborhood of well-tended little houses built after World War II. But now the neighborhood had fallen on hard times, and the owners of this house, the children of former occupants who were now in a nursing home, were more than happy to collect any rent at all.

"This is what we've got so far," Jimenez said. Jimenez was a third-generation Chicano, a short, pudgy family man who dressed like an office worker, a highly skilled computer hacker who never handled a gun.

"We've pushed this one as far as they'll go," Philip said. "Tell them to deposit the bitcoin and send us the specs."

"Sure we can't get a little more money out of them?" Jimenez asked.

"They're dragging their feet. We don't want them to start thinking about what they're doing. Get them to pay today."

"You're the boss."

"How many does that make this week?"

"Three. We've cleared seven grand apiece."

"I still can't believe how easy this is," Carrie said.

"Easy for you," Jimenez replied. "You're not dealing with this slow-as-molasses Tor browser."

The Travelers were running a dark web murder-for-hire scam. They'd been on the lookout for a fresh score when Jimenez got in touch with them about this scheme. Since they only stole from other criminals, finding the right job—a job that balanced pay and risk—was often difficult. But conning wannabe criminals was right up their alley, so they changed their names once again, got new IDs, and rolled into town.

Jimenez took care of the technical end: he set up the website—Death Becomes You—ran the transactions, communicated with the suckers, and collected the fees. The number of people who wanted to murder their spouse, coworker, business partner, or parents and were stupid enough to believe they could hire a stranger on the internet to do it seemed to be endless. The trick was not to seem too eager to take the job.

Philip and Carrie provided security, evaluated the marks, and ran the negotiations. Too many questions—When exactly will you get here? How long will you track the target? How do I know you won't cheat me?—was a definite deal breaker. The ideal mark knew just enough to arrange for the bitcoin and seemed to believe the rules for this transaction were just like the rules for any other online purchase. The typical ask was to kill a particular person who lived at a particular address and worked at another address, but don't harm their husband/wife/child/dog. Obviously a family spat. Why couldn't they just get a divorce? Or empty the bank accounts and run? How they planned to explain why their loved one was murdered by a stranger was simply not something they were thinking about.

The basic fee was $5,000 in bitcoin, but Philip and Carrie were always willing to wring more cash out of a mark if the mark wanted something special—poison, a car crash, a fall from a high place—or needed an expedited timeline. The deeper the client dove into the fantasy of murder, the easier it was to extract extra cash. As soon as the client transferred the bitcoin, Jimenez sent a series of messages pretending to set up the kill. Then he broke contact. When the mark sent further messages, he ignored them.

Carrie took a sip of coffee. "Did you hear back from Lucky Loo?"

"Yeah," Jimenez said. "He's all in."

"The whole ten thousand?"

Jimenez nodded.

"Let's have a look," Philip said.

Jimenez brought up the message stream on the screen. Lucky Loo was requesting an expedited kill, to look like a drug overdose, on Robin Simons, crime-beat reporter at the *Cornwell Herald* in Cornwell, Indiana.

"This reads like a mob hit or an FBI sting," Philip said.

"Mob wouldn't farm out a hit on the dark web," Carrie said.

"Which makes it look more like the FBI."

"If they pay, it doesn't matter," Jimenez said. "We're not killing anyone."

"Conspiracy doesn't require completion," Carrie replied.

Jimenez shook his head. "Conspiracy to commit murder, not conspiracy to create a fantasy."

"There's absolutely no way they can trace the bitcoin?" Philip asked.

"None."

"But they could find us?"

"It's possible," Jimenez said. "But that still won't take them to the bitcoin. What are you worried about?"

"What if it's the FBI?"

"Is creating a fantasy against the law? There's no crime without a victim. Who's going to press charges? *I hired them to kill my husband and they cheated me?*"

"Maybe you've got a clean sheet. But if the FBI takes us into custody, it won't take them but a few minutes to find a reason to hold us."

"Point taken."

"Can you find Lucky Loo's IP address?" Carrie asked.

"Carrie, the dark web is designed to keep you from being able to do that."

"But can you do it?"

"Yeah, I've got a program that will do that, but it's a brute force hack. It would probably take a few days on the equipment I have here. But why bother?"

"We could always just walk away," Philip said.

"Walk away from ten grand?" Jimenez asked. "Ten grand just waiting to be scooped up?"

"We need to find out who Lucky Loo is," Carrie said, "check them out, make sure we can't get stung."

"If the IP address leads us to a legitimate mark," Philip continued, "maybe we can milk them for even more cash. If not, we move on."

"Okay," Jimenez said. "I think it's overkill, but I'll get started on it."

TWO DAYS LATER, they had a file developed on Lucky Loo, AKA John Pollock, dentist. He lived at 687 Quail Run Trail in Cornwell, Indiana. He had a solo practice—Gentle Touch Dental—out by the megamall. His wife, Isabel, was a pretty, dark-haired woman who looked like she spent time in the gym. They had two kids, a boy and a girl.

"Open the Google Maps' view of the house again," Philip said. It was a large, two-story brick house situated among several streets of similar houses. "This is your regular vanilla salaryman's house."

Carrie nodded. "Maybe we've got him wrong. Maybe he's having an affair with the reporter and she's threatened to tell his wife."

"You've seen a picture of him and a picture of her. You think she's having an affair with him? This bozo is lucky his wife is sleeping with him."

"So, guys, is it a go?" Jimenez asked.

"It looks like a safe score," Philip said, "but we've got to be sure."

"I'll go check him out," Carrie said.

"That's going to cut into our profits," Jimenez said.

"It'll be worth it to know for a fact," Philip replied.

THE NEXT DAY, Carrie drove out of the Cornwell International Airport in a rental Nissan. It was a beautiful sunny afternoon. The map app on her phone directed her through the downtown to Sweetwater Boulevard, where she took a left and drove north past the Cornwell Technical College campus to Makepeace Valley Shopping Mall. In a strip mall across from the main mall entrance, she found her address. Gentle Touch Dental. She spotted a Wendy's across a side street, rolled through the drive-through for a Coke, and circled back around to park in the far corner of the Gentle Touch Dental parking lot, where she had a clear view of the front door.

She picked up her phone and called Philip. "Hey, baby."

"How was the flight?"

"They closed the Ben & Jerry's at O'Hare."

"I thought they had Haagen-Dazs."

"Well, they don't have either now."

"I'll pick up a pint of Coffee Chip for when you get back."

"Thanks."

"You find the place?"

"I'm in the lot."

"See anything of interest?"

"Not yet."

"Call me when you get to the hotel."

Carrie scooted down in her seat, sipped her Coke, and watched the front of the building. A couple pulled up in a rusty Dodge minivan. An elderly woman with a limp got out of the passenger's side and went into the dentist's office. The man, young enough to be her son, sat behind the wheel, smoking a cigarette. Ten minutes later the woman came out, and they drove away. Over the course of the next three hours, eight people came to Gentle Touch, but only two stayed there more than a few minutes.

At 5:00 p.m., a receptionist, a dental assistant, and Dr. John Pollock came out of the building and got into their cars. He looked exactly like the picture on his website—steel-gray hair, ears sticking out from his head, a deeply cleft chin. Carrie followed him north into Pheasant Ridge Estates—the neighborhood looked just like it did on Google Maps—where she parked on the street across from his house and watched him pull into the garage. Nothing to see here. She drove back across town to the airport and pulled into the Marriott Hotel. When she got into her room, she called Philip.

"He's definitely a dentist, but lots of people are coming and going who aren't in the office long enough to be having work done. Something sketchy's going on."

"Couldn't be the receptionist working under the table?"

"Not on her own. This is a three-person office. Everybody's got to be in on whatever's going on."

"But no cops?"

"No cops."

"It would make more sense if he wanted his wife killed."

"Like I said, he's up to no good."

"Okay. We'll see how much money we can get out of him. When you getting home?"

"I'm taking an early flight, connecting through O'Hare again, so I should be in Denver by three thirty. I'll send you the flight info."

"See you tomorrow."

"Love you."

"Love you more."

THE NEXT AFTERNOON, Philip, Carrie, and Jimenez were all back at the computer in their tiny rental house looking at their message stream with Lucky Loo.

Philip turned to Carrie. "This is what we did yesterday evening."

Their message: *You want the trifecta. A local celebrity, an ultra-short timeline, and a death that appears self-inflicted. Lots of expenses, lots of risk on a job like this. $10,000 won't quite get it done. Need $12,000.*

Lucky Loo: *This is crazy. You said $5,000. $10,000—that's double—definitely covers the extras. She's not really a celebrity.*

Their message: *You want the job done right—with no blowback—that's $12,000.*

Lucky Loo: *Okay. But not a penny more.*

Their message: *Move the bitcoin to the account and we'll begin work.*

Lucky Loo: *Half up front?*

Their message: *All or nothing. Looking forward to receiving payment and completing your job.*

Carrie leaned back in her chair. "Did he send the twelve thousand?"

Jimenez nodded. "I've already started the automated progress reports."

"This guy's a piece of work," Philip said. "They don't come any stupider. Wonder what the reporter's got on him?"

"Like I told you yesterday, there's something sketchy going on at his office," Carrie replied.

Jimenez logged out of the Tor browser. "Ready to twist the blade?"

"Have at it," Philip replied.

Jimenez pulled up a phony Russian email account and sent an email to the police department in Cornwell, Indiana, saying that someone had taken out a murder contract on Robin Simons.

"Well," Carrie said, "that one was actually kind of fun. It was nice to get out of town for a change."

Jimenez glanced at his watch. "Whoa, I'm running late. I've got to take my son to his soccer game."

"Can't your wife take him?" Philip asked.

"She doesn't do the sports stuff."

"What about the bitcoin?"

"I'll come back later and move it."

Jimenez rushed out the front door. Philip and Carrie walked

through the other rooms methodically and looked into the backyard for any indication that anyone had been on the property before they set the perimeter alarm and exited onto the street.

"What do you want to do tonight?" Carrie asked.

"We've still got to settle on another job."

"This one's going pretty well."

"It pays bills, but it won't send us on vacation for six months."

She laughed. "Too much like a day job?"

"It's exactly like a day job. We need to find a big money scam, let Merlin run the day-to-day on this—he's perfect for the job. Besides, it's not going to last forever. It's just like those scam emails offering to give you a million dollars. Eventually everyone except dementia patients figures it out."

"But in the meantime?"

"We're going to ride this money train."

THREE DAYS LATER, in Cornwell, Indiana, Robin Simons was leaning back against Detective Joel Marcos's blue Dodge Charger in the sweltering heat, talking to her editor on the phone while she waited for Marcos to come out of the courthouse. The day was more like August than June. Her blonde hair hung limp around her shoulders, and her tan pantsuit needed to be pressed. She examined the fingernails of her free hand. One nail was chipped.

"Yeah, Tim, court's about to let out, so Marcos and Bledsoe ought to be coming out the door any minute."

A group of people swarmed out of the courthouse and down the steps, Marcos and Bledsoe among them. "Got to go."

She smiled and waved. Marcos gave a little nod. He was a tall black man with a military haircut. He took off his necktie as he was walking down the steps and put it in the pocket of his gray suit coat. His partner, Steve Bledsoe, blue blazer and khaki slacks, bounced down the steps beside him with his hands out in front of him like a boxer practicing his moves.

"Hey, Robin," Marcos said. "What's up?"

"Looking for a comment."

"You heard what I said on the stand."

"You can't give me a tidbit for my editor?"

Bledsoe chuckled. "He's guilty. That's why we arrested him."

She rolled her eyes.

"Robin," Marcos said, "you know the drug task force can't comment on an open case. You need to talk to the DA."

"He's not talking."

"There you have it."

She shifted up off the car. "One other thing."

"Shoot."

"Have you got anything on that OD from last night?"

He shook his head. "Looks like the same counterfeit OxyContin we've been warning everyone about. Too much fentanyl in the mix."

"Off the record?"

"Honest, Robin, that's all we've got right now. Guy was off work on disability. Family man."

"So it's like a lot of the others we've been seeing lately."

Bledsoe ran a hand through his muddy brown hair. "Too many of them."

"Anything else?" Marcos asked. "We've got to go."

"Sure you can't give me a teeny little quote?"

He shook his head. "I'll see you at Sammy's."

THAT EVENING AFTER SUPPER, Dr. John Pollock sat in his home office at his computer logged on to his Tor browser. His last message to Death Becomes You had bounced back. Why couldn't he find them? They claimed to have done the job, and yet he knew that Robin Simons was still alive. She'd been following him around town, watching the dental office, harassing his patients. If she found out that he was selling OxyContin out of his dental practice, he'd be ruined. No one would believe his side of the story. Sure, he made money selling the pills. But these patients all had serious pain—pain that was never going away. So he wasn't a bad guy, not really. It wasn't like he was selling pills to kids or drug addicts.

When he'd first opened his dental practice, it had been so hard to find patients. He had dental school loans, equipment loans, the mortgage on his house. He was so depressed he could barely put one foot in front of the other. Then that first patient had shown up wanting a prescription for OxyContin. He paid for the office visit and left with the prescription. Soon the word got out. More patients appeared. He started to make some income to supplement his dental patients, but there were only so many prescriptions he could write without putting his dental license at risk.

And that's when he met Dylan Anderson. It had seemed at the time like a chance encounter, even though Anderson knew all about the prescriptions he was writing. One thing led to another. He started buying the pills from Anderson, selling them directly to his patients who needed them. He didn't have to risk writing OxyContin prescriptions anymore. And he made enough money to pay his bills while he built up his practice. But somewhere along the way, it became clear that Anderson wasn't really his friend, that he expected him to sell more and more pills, and that if he got caught, Anderson was going to blame him and expect his silence, even if he went to prison and lost his family.

So Robin Simons had to be hushed up. He didn't want to do it. He felt bad about needing to do it, but it was him, his wife, and his kids, or her. She didn't have to poke her nose in his business. She could have been investigating someone else. That was a choice she made. She'd brought this all on herself. If he could only get rid of her without Anderson finding out. God only knew what he'd do if he thought he was at risk. Maybe he'd misunderstood the timeline. Maybe Death Becomes You was still on the job. Maybe Robin Simons would commit suicide in the next few days.

"There you are."

He swiveled his chair toward the door. His wife, Isabel, a strand of dark hair hanging down in front of her ear, stood in the doorway with her hands on her hips. "You promised no working after supper."

"It was just one little thing I forgot about."

"It can wait until tomorrow."

"Sorry." He turned off the computer. He hoped he hadn't been duped. He hoped Robin Simons was still going to die.

ROBIN AND MARCOS sat in a wooden booth in the back of Sammy's Pizzeria, an old-fashioned pizza restaurant east of downtown where they both knew the owner. They were almost finished with their beers and an olive, mushroom, and pepperoni pizza. Joni, Sammy's teenage granddaughter, her apron splattered with tomato sauce, had just stopped by to check on them.

Marcos sipped his beer. "You still on the drug story?"

She sniggered. "I was waiting for you to ask. Tim has got me coming at it from the other end. Overprescribing and overdose deaths."

"And?"

"I'm in the same situation as you, Joel. Leads are hard to come by. Dead people can't talk, and people who are getting their pills don't want to talk."

"Tell me about it. We've got nothing but dead ends. Have you made any progress at all?"

"Nothing I can share."

"Really?"

She shrugged. "It's not that juicy."

"But we are helping each other out here?"

"Always. I just have to make sure that the *Herald* breaks the story ahead of the TV stations."

He took another sip of beer. "Always a pleasure talking shop with you, even when you're not telling me anything."

She smiled coquettishly.

"Have you got an early morning?"

"Nothing until nine. Want to come over?"

. . .

Over the next few days, Pollock obsessively checked the local news on his smartphone, but nothing had happened to Simons and he still hadn't gotten any replies to his emails to Death Becomes You. Where were they? If they could just get this job done, Simons would be off his back and his life could get back to normal. Being busy at work was a relief. He'd just finished with his last morning appointment—a simple bicuspid filling—when he got a call on his smartphone. It was Anderson. What could he want?

"John," Anderson said, "we need to meet."

"How about after work? Say, around five thirty?"

"How about now? You have to eat lunch, don't you? Meet me at the Barbeque Shack on Fulton Ave."

Pollock got into his BMW and drove into the old part of town south of the Cornwell Technical College. Three blocks past the campus, the Barbeque Shack sat between a used car lot and a Jiffy Lube. It was an old, white cinder block building. A row of picnic tables sat under an awning out front. Smoke wafted from the chimney at the back of the building and the air smelled heavily of roasting meat. When he got out of his car, he spotted Anderson seated at the picnic table farthest from the order window. Anderson had a stocky build, thinning hair, and the thick forearms of a man who'd spent years working with his hands. The man who brought the pills and took the money from his office, a tall man with slicked-back hair who was chewing with his mouth open, was sitting with Anderson.

"Sit down, John," Anderson said. "You remember Travis Smith, don't you?" He didn't wait for Pollock's reply. "We already ordered for you. Hope you don't mind."

Pollock sat down across from Anderson and Smith. Smith pushed a paper plate of pulled pork, collard greens, and French fries toward him. "The lunch special," he said.

"Thanks," Pollock replied.

Smith shrugged.

"I don't mean to be rude," Pollock said, "but why am I here?"

"We found out you have a problem," Anderson said.

Pollock looked at him quizzically.

"The reporter?"

"I'm taking care of that. I wanted to keep you out of it."

"Really? What did you do?"

Pollock explained.

Anderson shook his head like he was listening to a dim-witted child. "Remember I told you we like to keep everything close?"

Pollock nodded.

"That you should come to me with any sort of problem?"

"But I just thought it would be better if there was no local connection."

"You just thought? What's the most important rule?"

"Don't tell anyone anything."

"Do your employees know what's going on?"

"No, they just do their jobs and enjoy their bonuses."

"Exactly. That's how it's supposed to go. So before we had the reporter to deal with. Now we've got the reporter and these other assholes."

"But they don't know anything."

"They know you want the reporter dead."

"They can't find me. I was using a Tor browser on the dark web."

"You watch too much TV. Of course they can find you. It's just hard to do. What's to stop them from blackmailing you from here on out?"

"What do you want me to do?"

"You're going to bring me the internet address and all the emails you've got for these murder-for-hire assholes. You're going to do that today. Travis will come by your office to pick them up."

"The info's at my house."

"Then stop by your house. I want the info this afternoon. I'll put my tech guy on it. He'll find them. We'll deal with them first, then the reporter. Nice and easy. No loose ends. But you're going to pay for the contractor because you screwed this up."

"But I'm already out twelve thousand."

"And that's what it cost you to learn your lesson. In the meantime, keep your head down. We don't want any more trouble." He pushed up from the table.

"Enjoy your lunch," Smith said.

Anderson and Smith dumped their trash into the barrel at the corner of the building and got into Anderson's Cadillac. Pollock watched them drive away. How did Anderson find out? Who could have told him? Who else knew? He pushed his lunch plate away. Why couldn't he catch a break just this one time?

ANDERSON TOOK A LEFT at the first intersection. Smith glanced back at Pollock as they turned the corner. "Do you want him cleaned up?"

"No. He's an idiot, but he's a steady earner. We've never lost a dime on him."

"Put Little Jim on this problem?"

"Yeah. And as soon as he has the info, you can call that contractor we used last year."

"Consider it done."

WHEN POLLOCK GOT to his house, he parked in the driveway and went up the steps and through the front door. The neighborhood was quiet, all the kids at school and the parents at work. It would be a few more hours before the afternoon hubbub began and the stay-at-home moms started their afternoon chauffeuring.

"Honey?" he yelled.

There was no answer. Maybe she was out somewhere. Better if she didn't know he'd been home. He sat down at his desk in his home office and turned on the computer. Where were those emails and the website address? He opened the Tor browser and copied the information onto his desktop.

"John."

He swiveled in his chair. Isabel was standing in the door, wearing yoga clothes and carrying a basket of laundry. "What are you doing home?"

"Just had to do a few emails." He closed the Tor browser.

"Is something wrong?" She came into the office and set the laundry basket on his desk.

"No, no, just trying to be more efficient with my time."

"You're not a very good liar. Are you being sued again?"

He stood up. "Sued? No, absolutely not. Nothing like that."

"Well, something's up. You've been preoccupied the last few weeks, moody, haven't been taking an interest in the kids or me. And you've been hiding in here emailing someone you don't want me to know about."

He came around the desk. "Honestly, Isabel, nothing's going on. I'm not being sued. I'm just a little overextended financially. But I'm sorting it out. Everything's going to be fine. It's just going to take a few more weeks."

She studied his face. "Is that really the truth?"

"Really."

"I've been so worried. When you didn't want to have sex the other night—"

"You thought I'm having an affair?" He kissed her. "Isabel, you've got nothing to worry about. You're my only one. You and the kids are everything to me."

"Do you mean it?"

"Yes." He kissed her again. "Look, I need to finish up here and get back to the office. But tonight, after the kids go to bed, you'll have my undivided attention."

She picked up the laundry basket. "I'm going to hold you to that."

"I hope so," he replied.

2

ON THE HUNT

Four days later, at 5:15 p.m., Jimenez sat at the desktop computer in the stucco house, cleaning up some files and waiting for Philip and Carrie to come back with takeout Chinese. They had two more prospects to look over this evening. His plan was to get them set and then take a three-day weekend with his family in the mountains near Estes Park. He heard the door open, turned in his seat, and called out. "Hey, guys, it's about time."

A man in jeans, boots, and a black jacket appeared in the doorway, lifting a pistol as he walked into the room. Jimenez reached for his phone. "Who the hell are you?"

The man shot Jimenez twice in the chest. Jimenez fell backward out of his chair. The man turned out of the room. Jimenez lay panting, his blood sopping through his shirt, his phone still in his hand. He speed-dialed Carrie.

"We're about to pull up," she said.

"Killer inside," he gasped.

Carrie turned to Philip. "Merlin's been shot. Somebody's in the house."

Philip pulled to the curb in front of the little house. The neighborhood was quiet. The front door was shut. There was nothing out of the ordinary about the front yard. He glanced up and down the street at the parked cars. "Nobody's out here."

"He's waiting inside."

"One guy?"

"According to Merlin."

"Who might still be alive. I'll take the front, you take the back."

Carrie slipped out of the Cadillac and crept along the holly bushes that ran between their house and the next-door neighbors, her Glock down at her side. Philip counted to twenty. Then he came out of the car and walked straight up the sidewalk to the front door, a large sack of takeout in one hand and his Smith & Wesson .38 in his other hand. When he reached the door, he noticed that it wasn't quite shut. He pushed it with his foot, letting it glide softly open. No one was in the empty living room or the hallway. He moved through the house as if he was completely clueless. "Hey, Merlin, this place didn't have the Kung Pow chicken."

A tall man wearing a black jacket turned out of the bathroom with a pistol raised up in front of him and fired twice. Philip dropped to the ground, the bullets whizzing over his head, and fired upward. The back door crashed in. The man glanced over his shoulder just as Carrie was hurrying through the kitchen, firing as she came. "Stay down," she yelled.

Philip flipped onto his back and fired up into the man's belly. The man careened sideways into the wall and slid down to the floor.

Carrie stepped by him. "You okay?"

Philip got to his feet. Chinese food was mashed into his shirt. "I'm good. Where's Merlin?"

They found Jimenez in the office. Philip put a finger on his neck. "He's dead."

Carrie glanced toward the front of the house. "We've got what? Four or five minutes?"

"Computer, phones, leave the monitor."

"What about Merlin?"

"Lease is in his name, so he stays."

"The shooter?"

"We take him with us. Whoever hired him needs to think he's still moving."

Philip put Jimenez's phone in his pocket, pulled the cables from the back of the computer and passed the computer to Carrie. "Go have a look." He handed her his car keys. She went down the steps into the yard. They'd chosen this location wisely. No one was peeking out their windows. She put the computer in the trunk.

By the time she got back inside, Philip had the killer propped up on his feet, his belt tied around his thighs to stabilize his legs. "Wish his jacket was longer."

She shrugged. "Clock's ticking."

They walked the killer down to the Cadillac, looked up and down the street, popped open the trunk, and tipped him inside. "Drive around the corner onto Milton," Philip said. "I'm going to check things over."

She got in the car. He jogged back up to the house. All the rooms were empty except for the bedroom they'd been using. Bathroom—no trash. Hallway—killer's blood and a smashed bag of Chinese take-out. Their office—folding table, monitor, computer cables, no trash, Merlin. Philip went through Jimenez's pockets. His wallet contained the usual items, including a driver's license with his real name and address. The cops would have no trouble finding his family. What a way to live. Philip patted Jimenez's cheek. Goodbye, buddy. We'll make this right for you.

He wiped down the surfaces in the room and the doorknobs throughout the house. Back out in the hall, he stopped and read the side of the leaking takeout sack. Big Ma's Real Chinese. He wasn't going to take the chance that someone remembered them at the restaurant. He picked up the sack, left out the back door, cut across the neighbor's backyard, and walked by the rose bushes that ran along the sidewalk beside the detached garage. He sauntered down to the corner. Their Cadillac was idling on the street two houses down. He dropped the takeout sack into a trashcan that had been pulled out to the curb.

They drove northwest into the mountains, driving up switchbacks, looking for a parking area with a dumpster that overlooked a fast-moving river rapids. It was dark by the time they found one where no one was parked. They pulled up beside the dumpster. "Let's see who we've got," Philip said.

Carrie popped the trunk. The dead body smell of blood and shit wafted up. They turned on the flashlights on their smartphones. The killer lay like a ragdoll, his head flopped to one side and his arms bent at odd angles. "Asshole," Philip said. He handed his phone to Carrie. "Hold the lights."

Philip went through the killer's pockets. Nothing but a burner phone. "He must have left his keys in his car."

Carrie handed Philip his phone. "Professional."

"Yeah. Doesn't matter, though. We know who did it."

"The hit on the reporter?"

"Has to be it."

"If that's it, and Pollock could hire a pro, than why did he hire us?"

"That's one of the things we're going to be finding out."

She looked down at the killer. "Dumpster or the river?"

"Your call."

"Dumpster's right here."

"How full is it?"

She flipped open the lid. "Plenty of room. Must have been emptied yesterday."

"I'll take the head," Philip said.

"Thanks, sweetie."

They dragged the killer out of the trunk, gave him a few swings to gain momentum and heaved him into the dumpster.

"Let's get out of here." Carrie pulled the trunk lid back down.

"I'll drive," Philip said.

They started back down the mountain, heading for the apartment where they'd been living, Philip taking it easy on the switchbacks, the occasional car passing them on the straightaways.

"Glad to be rid of that bastard," he said.

"The trunk's a mess."

"We'll need to bleach it before we dump it."

"We going after them?"

"Merlin was a gentle guy. Never hurt anybody. He's got a wife and three kids. We were supposed to provide security. We owe him. And Pollock screwed up our scam, so he owes us for that, too."

"So we're going to get payback for Merlin, and we're going to figure out what Pollock's game is and rob him. Split the money with Merlin's family."

"He was our partner, so he keeps his share."

She looked out the window at the pine trees sliding by in the dark. "Pollock hired us and he bungled the negotiation. That make him a clueless bastard. There's no way he sent someone after us. I wonder who he's connected with. Think somebody's set up at our apartment?"

"No."

"Me neither. But let's go to a motel."

"You think Merlin might have said something to his wife? That his wife might have talked?" Philip asked.

"I just think we need to be extra careful."

"You remember that first time we used Merlin on a job?"

"He was a skinny little guy back then. Didn't really inspire confidence."

Philip chuckled. "Green as grass. But he proved himself."

"Yeah, worked his magic from the very beginning. I can't remember how we met him."

"He wasn't even married back then." Philip pulled up to a T intersection and turned right. "Are you carrying a burner?"

"Yeah."

"The reporter? What's her name?"

"Robin Simons."

"You have her information?"

"Sure. I picked it up in Cornwell."

"Let's tip her off. Put a little pressure on the dentist and his friends. See if that doesn't make our job easier."

Carrie got the burner phone out of her shoulder bag, looked up Simons's phone number on her smartphone, and made the call on the burner. She put the phone on speaker while the number rang.

"Hello?"

"Is this Robin Simons?"

"Who's calling?"

"John Pollock's put out a contract on you."

She laughed. "That's absurd."

"You've been warned."

"I don't believe you."

"Suit yourself."

"You can't scare me off."

Carrie hung up. "She's not buying it."

"We'll see." Philip stopped at an intersection and turned left. "Call Billy."

Carrie called Billy on her smartphone and put it on speaker. "Hey, Billy."

"Hey, missus. What can I do for you?"

"Billy," Philip said, "Our scam is blown. Merlin didn't make it."

"I'm sorry to hear that. I've got a good PO box for him where you can send his cut."

"That's great. But right now we need two sets of heavy gear. We'd want to pick them up in Cornwell, Indiana, in a couple of days."

"Hunting or running?"

"Hunting."

"I've got a guy in Chicago who can make that delivery in two or three days. I'll sent you the details as soon as I know."

"Appreciate it."

"Be safe."

Two days later, Philip and Carrie were parked facing out at the far end of an interstate rest stop south of Cornwell, Indiana, during an afternoon thunderstorm. The rain was coming down hard, bouncing off the pavement, tiny bits of hail pinging off the roof and hood of their Toyota Highlander. A man holding two small children by their hands ran from a minivan into the visitors' center.

"Hope our guy doesn't get here until the rain breaks," Carrie said.

"No such luck," Philip replied. "Here he is."

A red pickup truck with a matching camper top rolled into the rest stop. Philip flashed his lights. The truck backed in beside them. The driver was an older black man wearing a flat cap. Carrie and he lowered their windows. "We have a friend in common?" Carrie asked.

"Billy sends his regards."

Lightning cracked across the sky to the east and thunder boomed from a nearby field. The rain started to pick up. "Let's get this done," Carrie said.

Philip and the black man both hurried to the backs of their vehicles and raised the hatches. The black man slid a large duffel out of the truck and swung it to Philip. "That's the first," he said.

Philip nodded. The wind shifted, slanting the rain into his face. He shoved the duffel into the back of the SUV. When he turned, the black man was holding out a second duffel. "And that's the rest."

Philip grabbed the straps. "Have an easy drive."

The black man nodded and disappeared. Philip shoved the second duffel into the back of the Highlander and climbed in after it.

"You ready?" Carrie asked.

"Yeah."

Carrie pulled out and headed for the on-ramp, slowly gaining speed as she moved along. Philip opened the first duffel. Kevlar vest, AR-15 rifle, Glock pistol, Coms set, ammunition. Billy always provided the good stuff. He opened the second duffel. Another vest, another AR-15, another Glock, more ammunition, and a sniper rifle.

"How does it look?" Carrie asked.

"We've got the full kit."

"It came from Billy. What did you expect?"

"I know. I just had to check."

Philip climbed up to the front, his wet clothes sticking to his skin.

"You're soaked."

"I'll be okay." He took a hand towel from the glovebox and dried his hair. "Nasty weather makes for great cover." He tossed the towel into the back seat. "We've got the dentist and the reporter. Who do you want to start with first?"

"If our info is correct, Pollock is a direct link. He's doing dirt. At some point he's got to connect with some more bad guys."

"So we start with him. We've got to move quickly. Get things figured out and hit them before they realize we're here."

The rain stopped abruptly, and the sun was shining by the time they took the second exit into Cornwell. "Where to?" Carrie asked.

"Have we still got time to tag Pollock today?"

"Pollock it is."

She took Sweetwater Boulevard out to Makepeace Valley Shopping Mall and pulled into the parking lot of Jones Brothers Realty next door to the Gentle Touch Dental practice. It was 4:30 p.m. "They close at five."

Philip scanned the area. Normal traffic at the Wendy's, two empty cars in the Jones Brothers lot, no one parked on the street. Six empty vehicles in the Gentle Touch parking lot. "Nobody here but us. Let's see what their last thirty minutes looks like."

A young woman with a toddler on her hip, her wild hair in a loose ponytail, came out of the dental office and got into an old Ford. "Not a dental patient," Philip said.

"No."

A middle-age man dressed in khakis and a button-up shirt came out next, touched his cheek, and climbed into a Subaru. "Dental patient," Philip said.

"Definitely."

A thirty-something man with a significant limp, dressed in a ball cap and work clothes, came out of the dental office and got into a Dodge truck. "See what I mean?" Carrie asked.

"Must be moving drugs."

"But is Pollock a partner or a patsy?"

"I guess we'll find out."

A few minutes later, Pollock, his assistant, and the receptionist all came out together. The receptionist locked the door. They said their goodbyes and got in their cars. Philip and Carrie followed Pollock's blue BMW north. "He's heading home," she said.

They drove past his two-story house after he pulled into the garage, turned around in a driveway on the next block, and parked on the opposite side of the street about half a block down, where they had a good view of the front of his house: planters bursting with colorful flowers on both sides of the front steps, girl's bicycle lying on its side in the front yard, and a rolled-up newspaper lying on the driveway.

"Completely normal," Philip said.

"Just like all the rest of this neighborhood."

A few minutes later, a Ford Expedition pulled up in the driveway and a girl wearing soccer clothes got out of the back and ran up the steps. The SUV backed out and drove away.

"If he's a bad man, he's hiding in plain sight," Carrie said.

"Nothing's going to be happening around here," Philip replied. "Where do you want to stay?"

"How about the Quality Inn out at the interchange, at least until we figure out how long we're going to be here?"

"Okay. Let's go check in and find somewhere to eat. We'll get back on Pollock tomorrow."

The next day, Philip and Carrie shadowed Pollock all day, starting when he left his house in the morning. He went to work, took his employees to lunch, came home for supper, stayed in for the evening. No hard guys, no strip clubs, no sleazy bars, no girlfriend—nothing remotely of interest.

At 8:00 p.m., Philip and Carrie left Pollock's house and went to the Paradise Truck Plaza across the highway from the Quality Inn to eat supper. A Please Seat Yourself sign stood beside the hostess stand. They sat at a booth in the back corner. Their server, a black woman wearing a brown uniform, brought them water and menus. She smiled. "We're all out of the meatloaf special. Coffee?"

Philip and Carrie shook their heads.

"I'll give you a few minutes."

Philip ordered a burger, substituting a salad for the fries. Carrie ordered a chicken salad with the dressing on the side. After their server brought their food and disappeared, Philip said, "Pollock doesn't look very promising."

"We may have to watch him for a week."

"Or two. We don't know how the drop-off works. It could be one of the fake dental patients."

"Maybe," Carrie said. "But would you trust any of the ones we're seen thus far with cash or drugs?"

"No."

Carrie took a drink of water. "So what are you saying? Should we try the reporter or should we split up?"

"Let's try her out. Get the lay of the land. Then we can decide. It'll only cost us a day or two. Maybe we'll get lucky."

After they finished eating, Philip strolled out into the parking lot while Carrie went to the ladies' room. Rows of semitrucks were idling in the dark beyond the diesel pumps and the truck wash. As he reached their Highlander, a young girl in wrinkled clothes, maybe fifteen or sixteen, her shirt unbuttoned to show her bra, came out of the dark between two nearby trucks.

"Hey, Mister," she said.

"Hey yourself."

"You looking for some action?"

"How old are you?"

"Old enough."

"How do you know I'm not a cop?"

She grinned. "You're not a cop."

He looked her over. Her clothes were cheap and didn't fit well. She was underfed or on the needle. "Where's your purse?"

"Why are you asking?"

"You've got to have some way of carrying money."

"I've got pockets."

Just then, Carrie came around the corner. "What have we got here?"

The girl shifted around to look at both of them at the same time. "You're with him?"

"No worries," Carrie said.

"So that's how it is," the girl replied. "You want to watch, or you want me to do you, too?"

"Have you got any ID, honey?"

"What's up with you two?" the girl replied.

"Your man watching you?" Carrie asked.

"Maybe."

"Is this your chosen profession?" Philip asked.

"What do you mean?"

"'Cause I'm cool with it if this is how you make your way. But—"

Carrie cut in. "If you want to go home, we can hook you up."

"Why should I believe you?"

"You don't have to believe us," Philip said. "Just see what we do. You want to go home, get in the SUV." He turned to Carrie. "Let's go."

They got into the Highlander. Just as Philip was about to put it into Drive, the girl slipped into the back seat. "You better not hurt me."

Carrie turned in the seat to look at her. "That's not how we play this game, sweetheart."

They took her to the bus station, pulling through a MacDonald's drive-through along the way. The seats in the waiting area were worn, the pinball games were old, and the food choices at the concession stand did not look appetizing, but the bus station was clean, and the employees were professional.

"Where to?" Philip asked.

"Jacksonville, Florida."

"That's a long ride. You got any people who'd be happy to see you?"

"My mom."

"You got an ID to buy the ticket?"

She kicked off a tennis shoe and took an ID card out from under the insole.

Philip read the front. "Florida state ID. Makes you seventeen, if the ID is really yours, Linda."

They went to the ticket counter, where Philip purchased her ticket. "Your bus is at six a.m. Lots of time to change your mind."

"I won't change my mind."

He pulled a wad of cash out of his pocket. She eyed the money greedily. He counted out one hundred dollars. "Food money." He handed her the cash. "A lot of temptation. But it's up to you. You can take this chance to walk away or you can go back to the hell you've been living in."

"I'm leaving."

"Good luck," Carrie said.

Philip and Carrie left her in the bus station. "Think she'll leave?" Carrie asked.

"I don't know."

"Probably a bad idea to help her."

"I know. But I hate slavers. Bastards conning little girls, drugging them, using them, and then throwing them away. That's not a legitimate criminal activity."

"Preaching to the choir, baby. I just don't know if this will make any difference."

THE GIRL WATCHED them drive away. That guy didn't miss anything. She'd stolen that ID from one of the other girls. And who the hell were they, helping her and not wanting anything? She looked at the doors to the bus station. If Lincoln found her, she'd get a beating for sure. A long time until the bus. It would be stupid to wait here. She pushed through the doors out to the bus platform and walked off into the downtown. Three blocks over, top forty hits blared out of a bar on the corner. Small groups of drunk men and women congregated on the sidewalk, smoking cigarettes or vaping, laughing and flirting. The girl spotted a guy standing by himself at the entrance to the alley behind the bar. She sauntered up. "Got a cigarette?"

He shook one out of a pack he pulled from his pants pocket and lit it for her. "You working?"

"No."

"Then it's a little past your bedtime, isn't it?"

"I thought you were a good guy, but you're going to get me to change my mind."

He laughed. "Why are we talking?"

"You got any Oxy?"

"You got any money?"

"I thought we might trade."

"I don't need no STI."

"Ha, ha."

"If you don't want to make a purchase, you need to move along."

"Give me two."

"Thirty bucks."

She handed him the money. He whistled down the alley. A kid in old jeans and a sweatshirt, he couldn't have been more that fourteen, stepped out of the gloom. The guy flashed two fingers at the kid, who handed the girl two pills. She put them in her mouth and swallowed.

"See you around," the guy said.

"Uh-huh." She meandered through the groups in front of the bar, past the entry, and found a spot around the corner where she could sit on the sidewalk and listen to the music. She had plenty of time. She closed her eyes for a moment.

When she woke up, a pumped-up guy wearing a cowboy hat was kicking the sole of her shoe with his cowboy boot.

"Bar's closed. You've got to go."

She rubbed her face. "What time is it?"

"Three thirty."

She stumbled to her feet and started back toward the bus station. She felt in her pockets. She still had her remaining money and the bus ticket. The streets were deserted. When a car slowed down to check her out, she looked away. It sped back up.

She was the only one in the bus station. She went into the ladies' room, used the stall, washed her hands, and rinsed her face. When she came out, the man behind the counter said, "Ma'am? Do you have a ticket? You can't stay here if you don't have a ticket."

She walked up to the counter and pulled her ticket from her pocket.

"Thank you, ma'am. Your bus is on time. Six a.m."

She sat down in a chair next to the wall and closed her eyes.

THE SMACK across the face woke her. Lincoln stood over her. He was a fat man with a dark crew-cut, a tightly trimmed beard, and a crucifix tattoo on the back of his left hand. "Gypsy. What are you doing here?"

He grabbed her by the arm and pulled her to her feet. A gray-haired couple sitting near the door to the bus platform shrank back in their seats.

"I can explain," she said.

"I bet you can."

The man behind the counter called out, "Ma'am, ma'am, are you all right?"

Lincoln glowered down at her.

"I'm fine," she said. "Everything's fine."

Lincoln dragged her from the bus station. The morning was already bright. "Been looking for you everywhere. Thought you might have been hurt."

He pushed her into the back seat of a Suburban and got in beside her. Two big men with shaved heads, Carlos and Sergei, sat in the front. "Get out of here," Lincoln said.

Carlos pulled out into the early morning traffic. Lincoln gripped Gypsy's forearm and twisted her hand. She squealed. "Sunny saw you get in an SUV with a man and a woman."

"I thought it was business."

"Then why didn't you get out?"

She paused. He twisted her hand again.

"Please. Please."

He flipped her over in the seat and ran his hands through her pockets. "Seventy bucks and a bus ticket."

"I wasn't going to leave."

He punched her in the eye. "You're going to tell the truth eventually, so you might as well start now."

Carlos chuckled.

"The man and woman Sunny saw. They gave me the money and bought the bus ticket."

"That's better." He slapped her face. "Tell me everything that happened. Start when you left with them."

3

ROBIN SIMONS

At 9:00 a.m., Philip and Carrie were sitting in their Highlander in the on-street parking next to the Cornwell Herald building keeping an eye on the *Herald*'s parking lot. The Herald building was a five-story limestone rectangle located two blocks from the county courthouse to the east and five blocks from the convention center to the west. This far from the shopping and restaurants, the traffic was spare and there were only a few people waiting at the bus stop. A young woman, blonde hair, slim build, tan pantsuit, came out of the building and got into a white Camry.

"That's her," Carrie said.

They followed Robin Simons out of the downtown and into a neighborhood of small houses near the old train station. She pulled to the curb in front of a white clapboard house with peeling paint. They parked half a block back and watched her walk up on the porch and ring the doorbell. Someone cracked open the door and spoke a few words before they shut the door again. Robin got back in her car, drove east, avoiding the morning traffic, and parked on the street in front of a three-story, brown brick apartment building. She disappeared inside. Philip and Carrie circled the block and found a parking spot within eyesight of the front entrance. A few minutes later, Robin came back out.

"Tough day to be the crime reporter," Philip said.

Robin drove out to Roosevelt Avenue, took a right turn, and pulled into the parking lot of a Caffeination coffee shop three blocks later. Philip and Carrie followed her into the lot and sat in their SUV, waiting for her. After ten minutes, Philip said, "Why don't you take a look?"

Carrie pushed through the door and got in line to order coffee. The shop was about half-full, with customers scattered throughout the tables working at computers or using their phones. Carrie spotted Robin sitting at a table near the front window, talking on her phone, her laptop computer open in front of her. Carrie bought a regular coffee and sat at a table directly behind Robin where she could eavesdrop.

"How did I get your number? I followed you from Dr. Pollock's office last week and got your name from your address," Robin said. "I just have a few questions." She set her phone down, typed something into her laptop, and input a new number into her phone.

"Good morning. I'm Robin Simons with the *Cornwell Herald*. Can I ask you a few questions?"

"About your dentist, Dr. Pollock."

"No, nothing like that. This would be completely off-the-record."

"I can be there in fifteen minutes."

Carrie hurried out of the coffee shop while Robin was closing her laptop.

"What did you find out?" Philip asked.

She recapped what she'd overheard.

"She really didn't believe your warning."

"She definitely thinks Pollock's up to something."

"And that's why he wants her dead."

They followed Robin down Roosevelt Avenue and into a neighborhood of newer, upscale houses that eventually gave way to a few streets of rental houses next to the freeway—old cars in the driveways, kids' toys scattered in the yards. She parked in front of a duplex with dented aluminum siding and a patchy lawn. On the left side, a Chevy Malibu convertible with a torn top sat in the driveway. "Have we seen that car at the dental office?" Carrie asked.

"I don't know," Philip replied. "It sort of looks familiar."

They watched Robin walk up to the left side duplex.

ROBIN KNOCKED ON THE DOOR. A middle-age woman with pasty skin, her bathrobe hanging open over her wrinkled pajamas, opened the door. "Mrs. Crosby?"

The woman nodded. Robin followed her into the living room. The big screen TV was playing a morning news show with the sound muted. Mrs. Crosby sat down in a rocker-recliner and pointed to a worn-out sofa. A cereal bowl and an empty coffee cup sat on the coffee table. "Still early for me. Haven't tidied up yet."

Robin sat down and took her notebook out of her bag. "Thanks for seeing me."

Mrs. Crosby frowned. "I thought this was off-the-record."

"It is. This is just to help me keep the information straight. Nothing you say will go into my story."

Mrs. Crosby nodded.

"You're a patient of Dr. Pollock's."

"Yes."

"What is he treating you for?"

"My teeth. Had bad dental care in the past. I have painful teeth."

"That must be horrible."

"It is. Hurts terrible when I eat."

"Has Dr. Pollock helped you?"

"Nothing to be done, really, except to control the pain."

"I'm sorry to hear that." Robin made a note. "Do you get your medicine at the drug store?"

"No, right at Dr. Pollock's office. It's very convenient. Keeps me from making another trip."

"Do you have insurance?"

She laughed. "Insurance? Who can afford that? Look, I've had problems in the past. I just need my medicine. Dr. Pollock takes care of me."

"I understand."

"He's a good man."

"That's what I hear. Mrs. Crosby, do you know of any other people who buy their medicine directly from Dr. Pollock?"

"He's providing a service to the community."

"No one?"

Mrs. Crosby looked at the TV screen for a moment as if the sound were on. "Why, exactly, are you so interested in Dr. Pollock?"

"I'm just trying to understand his practice."

"You sound like you're trying get him in trouble."

"I just want to know the truth."

"Maybe you should leave."

"Are you sure you don't know anyone else who buys their medicine directly from Dr. Pollock?"

Mrs. Crosby pointed toward her front door. "I asked you to leave."

Robin put away her notebook. "Thank you for your time." She put her business card on the coffee table. "If you ever want to talk, here's my number."

PHILIP AND CARRIE watched Robin come out of the duplex. "She's looking chipper," Carrie said.

Philip started the Highlander. "She must have heard something she liked." He gave Robin a half-block head start and pulled out to follow her.

SHORTLY AFTER LUNCH, Anderson sat behind his desk in his office at the A-Okay Autobody shop, his smartphone on speaker, talking to the contractor he had hired to kill the murder-for-hire scammers. Smith sat across from him, listening quietly. "That guy you sent get his work done?"

"Problem solved. Check the Denver paper."

"What about the other thing?"

"Haven't been able to get in touch with my guy."

"Well, I can't wait. I'll have to make my own arrangements."

"Do what you've got to do."

Anderson ended the call. "Send them in."

Smith opened the door. Peanut Frazier, a big man with a bleach-blond mullet and a Mr. Peanut tattoo on his left forearm, and Little Jim Lee, a skinny Chinese American dressed in jeans and a T-shirt and carrying a laptop computer, came into the room and sat down. Smith closed the door and leaned against the wall.

"Jimmy," Anderson said, "Anything new?"

"That murder-for-hire website is unresponsive, boss."

"Unresponsive?"

"Nobody's answering."

"My contact said to check the Denver newspaper."

Lee opened his laptop, found the *Denver Post*, checked for a murder. "This looks like it." He passed the laptop to Anderson.

Anderson read the article. Ongoing investigation. Man murdered in empty house. Neighbors reported gunshots. No real details. "Maybe we got one of them." He pushed the laptop back across his desk.

"Maybe there was only one," Lee replied. "One guy could easily run that scam."

"It's never one guy. Keep an eye out. Either the others ran, or they're planning to cause us trouble."

Lee nodded.

Anderson turned to Frazier. "Peanut. Are you looking for a payday?"

"Always."

"Robin Simons has got to go."

"How do you want it done?"

"Make it look like a suicide."

"That'll be tricky."

"Can you do it, or do I need someone else?"

"I can do it, boss. I'm just saying—"

"Then we're done here. Talk to Travis if you need anything."

LATER THAT EVENING, Philip and Carrie sat in their Highlander watching Robin's house, a baby blue ranch in a neighborhood of well-kept-up, smaller homes near an elementary school. The streets were quiet, except for the occasional local coming home or going out. Following Robin in the later morning and early afternoon hadn't told them anything new. She was digging for dirt on Pollock, and she didn't believe she was in danger. Beyond that, they had no idea of what she was up to. So they'd gone out to dinner, and now they were waiting for her to come home, just to get a sense of her evening routine.

A dark-colored Nissan parked on the street in front of her house, and a big man wearing dark clothes and a ball cap, a backpack over one shoulder, walked up the steps to the house, took a few seconds at the door, and went in, although he didn't turn on the lights.

"That guy is in the business," Philip said.

"Made good time picking the lock."

"Might have a key."

Carrie shifted in her seat. "Do we warn her when she comes home?"

"We already warned her. If the guy was going to kill her, he didn't have to break in. Maybe he's going to be in and out before she gets home. Let's see what he does. Follow him when he leaves."

About forty minutes later, Robin turned into her driveway, the garage door went up, and she drove inside. The light went on in what was, presumably, the kitchen, then the living room. Ten minutes later, the living room went dark. The big man jogged down to his car at the curb.

"Have a look in the house," Philip said. "I'll follow him."

Carrie ran across the street. Through the kitchen window, she could see Robin collapsed on the floor. She ran around to the front, pulled on throwaway gloves, and tried the door. It was unlocked. She moved quickly through to the kitchen. Robin was lying between the sink and the island, pills scattered around her and an empty bottle of vodka lying on its side near her outstretched hand. Carrie knelt beside her and felt her neck for a pulse. Still alive. Should she interfere? Robin was a civilian. And she might be useful. Carrie pushed her onto her side and shoved two fingers down her throat. She vomited a pool of foul-smelling liquid. Her eyes fluttered. Carrie pounded her back, and then put her fingers down her throat again. She vomited some more. Carrie dragged her away from the vomit and checked her pulse one more time. It was stronger. She picked up the landline phone from the kitchen counter and input 911.

"911. What's your emergency?"

"Drug overdose. Hurry." She gave the address and lay the receiver down without hanging up.

Carrie glanced around the room. Robin's satchel and jacket were in the floor by the pantry, the floor had shoe scuff marks—the guy must have been hiding in the pantry to grab her from behind. She turned to the island. A typed note with no signature lay there. This guy was barely pretending to make Robin's murder look like a suicide.

Carrie left through the front door and walked casually down the sidewalk, pulling off her gloves and shoving them into her pocket as she went. Then she crossed the street at the end of the block and headed back toward Jackson Boulevard on side streets that emergency vehicles wouldn't be taking to get to Robin's house. When she was three blocks away, she called Philip.

"I'm still on our guy," he said. "What did you find?"

She filled him in.

"She's going to believe they're after her now. Think the cops will be fooled?"

"I can't see how." She heard the ambulance siren somewhere close by.

"I hate to leave you on the street, but I'm going to be awhile."

"I'm fine. I'll find a place to sit and call you back."

. . .

PHILIP FOLLOWED the Nissan to a city park, where it turned into the parking lot by the restrooms. He pulled into the on-street parking outside the circle of light that illuminated the park entrance and turned off his headlights. A few minutes later, a motorcycle turned right out of the park. When it crossed under the streetlight, Philip saw that the rider had the same dark jacket and backpack that the man in the Nissan had been wearing. He turned on his headlights and started out after him. The motorcycle drove the speed limit and never circled around or gave any indications that the driver was looking for a tail or making sure to shake one. No tradecraft at all.

On the other side of the public golf course, the motorcycle turned left onto a gravel road. Philip slowed down to give it a little more room. About half a mile down the road, past two other small houses, the motorcycle pulled into the driveway of a tiny house with a car and a pickup truck parked outside. Light poured out of the windows, lighting up patches of the yard. Philip drove by the house, turned around, and parked on the other side of the gravel road. He took a Glock from his glove box. Then he sneaked down to the little house, the gun down at his side, and slipped up to the closest window to peek inside. The kitchen was empty, but through the doorway to the living room he could see two men, a dark-haired man sitting in an easy chair, and a bleach-blond wearing a dark jacket, who was drinking from a beer can.

Philip sneaked back to the Highlander and drove away. When he got back on the main road, he put his phone on hands-free and called Carrie.

"Hey," she said.

"Where are you?"

"Best Donuts on Claymore Street."

"I'm coming to you."

"Where did you go?"

He filled her in.

"That's not much of a lead."

"It's a start."

. . .

BACK AT ROBIN'S HOUSE, her front door was open and two paramedics knelt over her, a white man with a crew cut and a black woman with cornrows, the woman checking her vital signs. "You really know her?" the man asked.

"It's Robin Simons. From the *Herald*."

"Who would have thought?" The man injected her with Narcan.

Robin's eyes fluttered open. She began to stir.

The woman held a stethoscope to Robin's chest. "That's what I want to hear."

Robin looked from one paramedic to the other. "What happened? How did I—where's the woman?"

"Easy, Robin," the female paramedic said. "We're the only ones here. You're on your kitchen floor. We got a 911 emergency call. Do you remember what happened?"

Robin was trying to take in what the paramedic was saying. "Someone broke into my house." She reached up and touched her mouth. "Are my lips bleeding?"

"Your lips are bruised."

"Someone attacked me."

The paramedics exchanged a glance. "We're going to take you to the hospital, so you can get checked out," the female paramedic said.

"Okay."

"Can you walk?"

"Yes."

She shuffled along, the female paramedic holding her arm and the male paramedic carrying their gear. While they were crossing the lawn to the ambulance parked in her driveway, Marcos screeched to a stop in the street and jumped out of his Dodge Charger.

"Robin!"

He ran to her and grabbed her by her shoulders. "Are you okay?"

"I don't know. I think so. Still woozy."

"We gave her Narcan, Detective Marcos," the male paramedic said.

"Somebody jumped me," Robin said. "They were in my house."

"Can I look inside?" Marcos asked.

Robin nodded.

"I'll see you at the hospital."

Marcos went up the steps into the house. The lights were on. He got out his smartphone and started taking pictures. The puddle of sick, the pills, the empty vodka bottle—Robin barely drank. He slipped on a throwaway glove and picked up the typed note from the island counter. Bullshit. He went to the back door and opened it. No sign of forced entry. This was going to be tricky. He called his partner.

By the time Bledsoe got there, Marcos had already checked all the windows and called dispatch to see if any complaints had been called in for this neighborhood over the last week. All the windows were locked tight and the neighborhood was quiet. Bledsoe glanced around the kitchen.

"You haven't touched anything?"

Marcos shook his head.

"She's your girl. You were here first."

"I know."

"You checked everything?"

"Yeah. No sign of a break-in."

Bledsoe read the note on the counter without picking it up. Then he got down on one knee and picked up a pill. "It's those counterfeit OxyContin that we've been finding all over town."

"Looks like it."

Bledsoe took a small envelope out of his pants pocket and dropped the pill into it. "I talked to the EMTs."

"And?"

"Just looked like another OD to them. They didn't see anyone. Didn't mention the note."

"Someone called 911."

"Yeah, but there's not really enough evidence here to open a case."

"That's a load of crap."

"That's the way it is, partner. What's she working on?"

"The details? We better go ask her."

. . .

Robin was already in a regular hospital room by the time Marcos and Bledsoe arrived at the Cornwell Medical Center. It was long after visiting hours, but no one at the nurses' station asked the detectives what they were doing on the floor. Marcos knocked on Robin's door.

"Come in," she said.

She was sitting up in her bed, her hair pulled back from her face. Her right eye was bloodshot, and her cheek was bruised. "How are you feeling?" Marcos asked.

"You guys could have waited until morning."

"You know better than that."

"Doc says I'm fine, Joel. They're just keeping me overnight while the drugs flush out."

"You know how you were found, right?" Bledsoe asked.

She nodded. "911 call. I was drugged."

"We need to ask you some questions."

"Fire away."

"You told the paramedics someone attacked you?" Marcos asked.

"Did I? That part's still blurry."

"But someone was in your house?"

"I'd just come home, come in from the garage, someone grabbed me from behind."

Marcos sat on the edge of her bed. "Take your time."

"What did you see?" Bledsoe asked.

"He was a big guy. Dark clothes. Ski mask. He tossed me down on the floor. Sat on my chest. I was fighting and kicking as hard as I could. Thought he was going to rape me." Her face flushed red.

"But he didn't," Bledsoe said.

"No, he pinched my nose and shoved a bottle into my mouth. I thought he was going to break my teeth. It didn't taste right. I had to swallow." She shook her head. "That's all I remember."

"But you called 911. Reported a drug overdose. Left the phone off the hook."

"No. I don't think so. I saw a woman—"

"The paramedic?" Bledsoe asked.

"No. A white woman. Dark hair. She was pounding my back. But that doesn't make sense, does it?"

"Are you sure you didn't call 911?"

"It couldn't have been me. I was out cold. The paramedics revived me."

"The 911 recording will tell us if it was her," Marcos said. He squeezed her hand. "So this guy was there to kill you?"

"I know it sounds crazy. But come on, Joel. You know me. I'm not depressed. I don't take drugs. I got an anonymous call last week warning me, but I didn't believe it."

"You got a call that someone was going to kill you?"

"Happens more that you'd think. Somebody angry about a story, too much to drink, it never amounts to anything."

"That tip," Bledsoe asked, "do you have it recorded?"

"No."

Bledsoe and Marcos traded glances. "Man's voice or woman's voice?" Bledsoe asked.

"A woman."

"Who did she say was after you?"

"John Pollock."

"Who the hell is he?" Marcos asked.

"He's a dentist."

"And you're investigating him?"

"I'm looking into pill mills as part of my story on the surge in drug addiction."

"How's he involved?"

"I've got nothing solid yet, but I think he's selling OxyContin out of his office."

"And that's why he sent someone to murder you?"

"Pollock? Come on, Joel, there's no way Pollock would be involved in a murder. He doesn't fit the profile."

"How do you know? You have any evidence?"

"Someone emailed the tip line," Bledsoe said, "a couple of weeks ago. Claimed someone was after you."

"Why didn't you tell me?"

"The email didn't name anyone. Lewis looked into it, but there wasn't much to go on."

"So there's been two tips," Marcos said. "You need to take action to protect yourself."

"I'll be fine."

"I'm not going to lie to you," Bledsoe said. "With the drug overdose and no sign of a break-in, if you don't give us something solid, there's not much we can do for you."

"What makes you think they'll try again? Look, my investigation is still in its early days. There's not really that much to tell."

"Then it won't be a problem for you to lie low until we have a chance to develop a lead," Marcos said.

"I can't do that. This story is a priority for the paper. If I'm not working it, Tim will just assign someone else."

Marcos turned to Bledsoe. "Will you give us a minute, Steve?"

Bledsoe left the room.

"You're not going to talk me out of doing my job," Robin said.

"I'm not going to try. Are you really okay?"

"I'm still a little shaken up. But I'll be all right."

"I'm going to be watching your house."

"You don't have to do that."

"Just until I'm sure you're safe."

"Don't get in the way of my investigation."

"Always the tough guy."

"I mean it."

He kissed her forehead. "I'm glad you're okay. Get some sleep. You're safe here."

4

WHEELING AND DEALING

Early the next morning, while Philip and Carrie were still getting ready for the day, there was a knock on their motel room door. Philip peered through the peephole. He saw the teenage hooker standing in the middle of the doorway, all by herself. She had a split lip and a black eye that had gone to greenish-gray. Philip called over his shoulder, “Honey, we’ve got company.”

Carrie stepped out of the bathroom, still in her robe, and picked up a Glock from the bedside table. Philip gripped the butt of the Smith & Wesson that was stuck in the back of the waistband of his pants and opened the door. When he did, two men stepped out from either side of the door—a fat man with his hair and beard close-cropped the same length and a bruiser with a shaved head and a Cyrillic word tattooed on his neck.

The fat man slapped the girl on the back of the head. “Is this the guy?”

“Yeah, that’s him.”

The fat man eyed Philip up and down. “You’d shoot me right here in broad daylight with the tourists watching?”

“Maybe.”

Shaved Head shifted his weight.

"Your leg moves another inch," Philip said, "and I'm putting two in your knee."

The fat man smiled. "This girl belongs to me. Maybe you made a mistake. Maybe you didn't understand. But you're going to stay out of my business from here on out or life will become very difficult for you and your woman."

"You went to all the trouble to find me just to tell me that?"

"Just another smart-ass who thinks he can change the world."

"Not so much."

"Keep being a funny guy and you'll find out what trouble is." He turned to Shaved Head and the girl. "Let's go."

Philip watched them get into a silver Suburban before he closed the door.

Carrie set her Glock back on the bedside table. "They banged her up pretty good. That kid will look like she's forty before she's twenty."

"She won't live that long. Should have watched her get on the bus."

"She made her choice."

"They've got her on drugs and fear. Slavers. Smug bastard with his muscle boy. Beating her and then making her work looking like that."

"There's nothing more we can do."

"I'd like to put a stick in his eye."

"We're a little busy now."

"You're right. But that doesn't keep me from wanting it." He glanced around the room. "We need to change motels."

"Let me get dressed."

They packed their bags and loaded them into the back of the Highlander. Philip looked around the parking lot. Cars with out-of-state license plates and a few work trucks, all empty. A middle-age couple with a preteen girl dragging along a few feet behind them came out of a room and headed toward the office and the complimentary breakfast. There was nothing that looked the least bit suspicious.

"Think we need to wipe down the room?" Carrie asked.

"Let's skip it. The cops around here aren't after us yet."

After they turned in their keycards at the office, they drove down Elm Street into town looking for a restaurant. "Traditional, ethnic, or contemporary?" she asked.

"You decide."

"How about that one?"

He pulled into the parking lot of the Eggplant Café and parked next to the building. The sign attached to the roof featured vegetables spilling out of a cornucopia. "This place has got 1972 written all over it."

"You said I could choose. Besides, the parking lot is full."

"Fair enough."

The restaurant appeared to be a local hangout, full of groups of customers dressed for work chatting over their breakfasts, but a waitress in a yellow uniform swung by the hostess stand after just a few minutes and led them to a table. They ordered the house omelets—avocado, tomato, and pepper jack cheese—with coffee and bacon on the side. They studied the other customers and made small talk until their waitress brought their food. Then Carrie said, "So the dentist is dirty, and somebody tried to kill the reporter."

"Pollock isn't in charge. He's a family man in way over his head. Somebody else is running the show."

"Agreed." Carrie sipped her coffee. "So what's our next move?"

Philip swallowed a bite of omelet. "Quickest way? Simons knows enough that someone wants her dead. We need to know what she knows."

"She owes us a favor."

"But she was drugged up. Besides, even if she remembers you, that doesn't mean she'll help us out. We need to build a relationship, one where she thinks we're doing more for her than she is for us."

"So we need to find her a story."

"Exactly."

Carrie watched two senior citizens scrape back their chairs and shuffle toward the cash register at the counter. She smiled. "This might be a reach, but what about if we put her on the sex traffickers?"

"Put them on the front page of the newspaper? That would really piss them off."

"But if we give her a front-page story like that, we might become her new best friends. And then she might want to help us out with Pollock."

"That would make it worth the risk of aggravating the slavers."

"It could cut down on the amount of time we have to stay here."

"But it might put the kid in a tight spot."

"Only if the fat guy thinks it's her fault. And why would he? He's got her completely under control. And the truck stop is a big place. She'll be trying to avoid us. If the pimp's going to blame anyone, he's more likely to blame us."

"Then we might have a fight on our hands."

"You afraid of the bald guy?"

He smiled. "Just outlining the problem."

"So?"

"Okay, let's push Simons toward the slavers. See if that won't get her to help us out."

WHEN ROBIN WALKED out onto the sidewalk in front of the medical center, the white-haired volunteer at the valet stand asked her if she needed her car brought out. She shook her head no. Just then, Marcos tapped his car horn and pulled up into the loading zone. He lowered his passenger window. "You been out here long?"

She climbed in. "Just came out the door."

"Are you okay?"

"Yeah, doc says I'm fine. I'm just dragging. Another cup of coffee, maybe."

Marcos pulled out of the loading zone, circled around in the driveway, and turned right. "Where are we going?"

"Home. Tim told me to take it easy today."

"I cleaned up your kitchen for you."

"You didn't have to do that."

"Didn't think you'd want to deal with that mess this morning." He took the next left onto Roosevelt Avenue. "Tim ask you any questions?"

"You mean, did he believe me?"

Marcos nodded.

"As much as the doctor did. Told me there was no shame in getting help if I needed it."

"But you're still working the pill mill story?"

"Thus far."

"The OxyContin scattered on your kitchen floor look like the same counterfeit Oxy we've been finding all over town. Are you sure Pollock's selling OxyContin out of his office?"

"I've talked with patients off the record."

"So somebody does want to hush you up," Marcos said.

"Pollock's getting his pills somewhere."

"If he's getting them from Anderson, that would explain a lot."

"Have you got anything new on him?" Carrie asked.

"Nothing. We know he's the drug kingpin, but we haven't been able to get anything to stick to him. Somebody else always takes the fall. You're not going to leave this alone, are you?"

"No, I'm not."

"What's your next move?"

"Honestly? I'm going to take it easy this morning and then chase down some phone leads this afternoon. I need one of Pollock's patients on the record. Someone believable. And some physical evidence would be nice. Then I can confront Pollock, get him to tell me where the pills come from. That's my plan."

"You think he'll tell you?"

"If I've got him dead to rights, it will be his only chance to tell his side of the story."

"You're taking a lot of risk."

"I'm a big girl."

"A big girl whose life was saved by a stranger. I listened to the 911 recording. That wasn't you. You need to set your home alarm all the time, not just at night."

"I know. That was a dumb mistake." She squeezed his hand. "I'm going to be a lot more careful from here on out."

MEANWHILE, at Cornwell City Park, Travis Smith, wearing sunglasses and a ball cap, sat with Peanut Frazier at a picnic table under a black maple. In the distance, a group of moms huddled together talking, while their preschoolers played in the sandbox near the playground equipment. Behind them in the parking lot, three young men rolled by on skateboards. Smith waited until they were out of earshot before he spoke.

"Simons isn't dead," Smith said.

"I did an ace job, Travis. The boss wanted it to look like a suicide, and that's what you got. She should have died. No way she called for help. She was out cold when I left. I laid her on her back so she'd suffocate if she threw up." He dropped his cigarette on the ground and crushed it out. "It's like somebody was watching, got there right after me."

"You've got to be more careful." He glanced at a car that had just turned into the parking lot. "Our guy at the hospital says the cops interviewed her. I don't care how you do it, but she's got to go."

"I need to let things die down for a few days."

"A few days?"

"You want it to look like a suicide, don't you?"

"Don't wait too long."

"Just a couple of days. The cops will ease up, and I'll finish the job."

THAT AFTERNOON, Philip and Carrie drove up to a different freeway interchange and checked into a Best Western with easy access to the freeway on-ramp. After they brought their bags inside their room, Carrie kicked off her shoes and scooted up the bed to sit against the headboard. "Let's give the reporter a call."

Philip looked into the bathroom before he sat down on the bed beside her. "Where do you think she is?"

"Let's try the hospital first."

Carrie got out a burner phone and called the hospital to ask if Robin Simons was taking visitors. She'd checked out. She tried Robin's home phone next. It rang four times.

"Hello," Robin said.

"Hey," Carrie replied. She put her phone on speaker.

"Who is this?"

"Just the girl who turned you on your side and put her fingers down your throat."

"You're her?"

"Yeah."

"Why were you in my house?"

"Saw that guy come and go. Thought he was up to no good."

"So you were watching my house?"

"Yeah."

"Why?"

"Tried to warn you that Pollock was after you, but you just weren't believing it."

"That was you?"

"Yes."

"So you were trying to save my life?"

"Not trying, did."

"Yeah, I guess that's right. I guess I should thank you."

"You're welcome."

"Why don't we get together? Have a little chat. You can tell me how you knew Pollock was after me."

"We could trade straight up. We'll tell you how we know what we know if you tell us everything you've found out about him."

"Why are you chasing Pollock?"

"Pollock—probably not Pollock, from the look of him, probably somebody connected with him—sent someone after us. A friend of ours is dead."

"Why should I believe you?"

"I get it. You don't trust us. Why should you? But maybe we can win your trust."

"How's that?"

"You're the crime reporter, right?"

"Yeah."

"We're guessing the Pollock story is a hard slog."

"So?"

"How about a quick story for the front page?"

"Go on."

"Did you know there's prostitution out at Paradise Truck Plaza?"

"There's always been prostitution at the truck plaza."

"Trafficking in underage girls? Children who are beaten and drugged?"

"I'm listening."

"You up for a show and tell? We show you who's who and you write the story."

"Why do you care?"

"When it's grown women making their own decisions, we don't care. But assholes enslaving children, that's not right."

"Hang on a minute. I have to think."

Carrie smiled at Philip. He patted her thigh.

A few minutes later Robin came back on. "Okay, I'll go with you. Where do you want to meet?"

"Are you up for tonight?"

"I'll be ready."

"We'll pick you up at your house at nine p.m. You'll be able to see who we are and know you're safe before you get in the car."

"See you at nine."

Carrie ended the call.

"Nicely handled," Philip said.

"We've got some hours to kill."

"We know the dentist is probably involved in drugs somehow. Is he a big fish or a little fish? If he's the big fish, the cash is hidden somewhere. Office, home, bank safe deposit box."

"We should get a look inside his house," Carrie said. "Maybe there's a safe there. And what about the killer? You followed him home last night. Shouldn't we have a look in his place?"

"Yeah, we should. Let's start there."

They drove across town to the gravel road out past the public golf course. During the day, the houses along the road seemed particularly rundown. Weeds in the ditches, rusty cars in the yards, broken porch railings, and roofs that needed to be re-shingled. At the third little house, the motorcycle was parked beside the steps, but the car and the pickup truck were gone. Philip parked in the same place he'd parked before, across the gravel road facing out, and he and Carrie moved nonchalantly up the drive to the four-room house as if they were expected.

"What's our plan?" she asked.

"We know one of them's a killer. Chances are the other is, too."

"Okay." She slipped her hand into her shoulder bag and gripped the butt of her Glock.

They looked in the kitchen window on their way around to the front porch. They couldn't see anyone. "Bet no one's home," he said.

He knocked. There was no noise inside. He took his lock pick set from his wallet, inserted the tension pick in the bottom of the keyhole and the rake pike in the top, and scrubbed the rake pick over the pins inside the lock while he applied counterclockwise pressure to the tension pick. When the pins were all forced clear, the bolt slid back into the lock. He might have taken thirty seconds. He slowly eased the door open. No booby trap wire. They walked through the house. In the living room, a sofa, a loveseat, and a coffee table strewn with snack trash and two PlayStation controllers all faced a huge TV. To the right, in the kitchen, the sink was loaded with dirty dishes and the refrigerator held take-out leftovers, orange juice and canned beer. In the two bedrooms, the beds were unmade, and clothes were strewn across the floor. In one bedroom, a pump shotgun lay on the floor under the bed. In the other bedroom, a loaded Colt .45 sat on the closet shelf.

"This is very sad," Carrie said.

"When they say crime doesn't pay, they were talking about these two."

"Have we got time for the dentist's house?"

"We'll be cutting it close."

They drove into town, took Sweetwater Boulevard north, and turned west beyond the shopping mall to arrive at Pheasant Ridge. They parked on the street across from Dr. Pollock's brick two-story house. "Will we get a chance?"

"If his wife picks up the kids from school, she's be leaving in a few minutes," Philip replied.

The garage door went up and a BMW SUV backed out onto the street. A good-looking woman, dark hair and sunglasses, was driving. "That's her," Carrie said.

"We've got fifteen or twenty minutes."

"If they've got an alarm system, I bet she didn't set it."

"Let's try the side door to the garage."

They crossed the street and walked up the side of the house. No camera above the door. Philip picked the lock. No alarm went off.

They moved quickly across the empty garage to the door to the house. It was unlocked. They moved fast, glancing in the rooms, looking for a safe. Nothing in the first floor office. Carrie went upstairs. Four bedrooms—guest, master, girl's, and boy's—all immaculate. No safe in the master closet. Carrie went back down.

Philip was in the basement, which was finished as a family room. In a closet system the length of one wall, he found a two-foot-tall safe. It was not a very good one. He opened his phone and pulled up a list of safe manufacturers' try-out combinations that he kept updated. Had Pollock bothered to change the combination after the safe was installed? He dialed the try-out combination and pulled on the handle. The door opened. Could Pollock be any more clueless? Wife's jewelry in their jewelry store boxes, car titles, mortgage papers, what looked to be around $5,000 in cash. Nothing unusual. He closed the safe, spun the dial, and scurried up the steps to the first floor where Carrie was watching out the front windows. "Safe was downstairs. Nothing out of the ordinary."

They left into the garage. As they were crossing to the side door, the garage door started to raise. They rushed out to the side of the house and stood there, listening to the wife and the kids as they got out and went inside, waiting for the garage door to go down. When the garage door thudded closed, they walked quickly back across the street, climbed into the Highlander, and drove away.

"That was a little tight," Carrie said. "Schools must be close by."

"Just a little something to get the blood pumping."

"There was nothing worth taking?" Carrie asked.

"Just a normal family safe. Five grand and some jewelry. Maybe we'll come back for the money later, but I didn't want to tip him off now."

"So we really haven't found out that much today."

"Except that the killer is probably a stooge, not a pro, and Pollock is keeping money at his dental office or in a bank box."

"But we don't know who ordered the hit."

"Yeah. Still don't think it's Pollock. He wasn't smart enough to change the try-out combination. But we need to get a look in his dental office."

"Let's go back to the motel and rest a bit before dinner."

"Want to pick up some coffee along the way?"

"That sounds like a great idea."

AT 9:00 P.M., Philip and Carrie pulled up into Robin Simons's driveway. The outside lights were on, illuminating the ten feet around the porch. She came out of her house dressed in jeans and a black jacket, and made a show of locking the deadbolt. Philip and Carrie got out of the Highlander and stood together by the front bumper.

Carrie smiled. "Hey."

Robin eyed them both carefully.

"I spoke to you this afternoon. Told you about warning you."

Robin nodded. "But you didn't tell me what you do for a living."

Philip shoved his hands in his pockets so that he looked as nonthreatening as possible. "Are you carrying a recording device? Is it turned on?"

"Not yet."

"So what do you think we do for a living? Speaking hypothetically, of course."

"Well, if you knew Pollock wanted to have me killed, and knowing that got one of your friends killed, and you're here sneaking around trying to find who did it, and you helped me when that guy attacked me, but you didn't stay around for the ambulance, that makes it sound like you're into something shady that blew back on you."

"You really are a crime reporter," Philip said.

"But you've got nothing to worry about," Carrie continued. "You know that, right? If we wanted to hurt you, I wouldn't have helped you. We would have just left you to die."

"So you've got an agenda around exposing these sex traffickers?" Robin asked.

"Of course," Philip said. "But it's a real story. It won't come back to bite you."

"But what you really want to know is what I know about Pollock?"

"As much as you want to tell us."

"I'm still thinking about it."

"Fair enough," Philip said. "Let's go get your story."

Philip and Carrie drove Robin out to the Paradise Truck Plaza and parked in the shadows away from the gas pumps and the building.

"What do you know about this scene?" Carrie asked.

"Honestly?" Robin replied. "Not much."

Carrie pointed at the building. "The world in there is civilization. People eating in the restaurant, buying snacks in the mini-mart, picking up a souvenir to take home. All sweet and above board. The world out there"—she pointed to the rows of semitrucks idling in the shadows—"is the wild west. Some guys are in their sleeper cabs reading books, sleeping, talking to their wives on their phones. Other guys are buying drugs, screwing hookers, moving stolen merchandise. Everybody minds their own business. Nobody talks. That's why the cops can't do much. Isolated busts, that's about it."

"And the working girls come in three basic flavors," Philip continued, "independent operators, independents with protection—"

"Pimps," Robin said.

"Pimps as business partners, and the trafficked, who are really just slaves."

"Why don't they run?"

"Intimidation, drugs, and brainwashing. Lots of reasons that don't make sense when you're free. You could google it. Be on the lookout for girls without money or ID."

"So you ready for the tour?" Carrie asked.

"Let me set my camera." Robin adjusted her digital camera for night photos without flash.

They got out of the SUV and walked quietly toward the parked semitrucks. When they got closer, they saw a clump of men gathered on one side of a pickup truck. Philip leaned over to Robin and whispered, "Drug slingers." Robin took a photo.

As they started down a row of parked semitrucks, they noticed a figure climbing out of a nearby truck. Robin took her picture as she tugged down her miniskirt before she walked away. Around the corner, they saw another woman climbing up into an open cab. Robin took her picture as a man's hand reached out to help her inside. At the end of that row, near an overhead light, Robin took a picture of a small woman leaning against a truck bumper to steady herself.

"Oh, hell," Carrie said. "You want to leave that one alone. She might be sixteen. We gave her a bus ticket two days ago."

"You know her?" Robin slung her camera strap over her shoulder and turned on the recorder on her smartphone before she took off toward the girl.

Carrie started after her. Philip put his hand on her arm. "It's better if we stay out of the way." They slipped into the shadows between two trucks.

The girl swayed as she turned toward Robin. She had bruises on her neck and a faded black eye. The top of her dress was unbuttoned. "Hey, honey."

"How old are you?" Robin asked.

The girl put her hand on Robin's shoulder.

"What's your name?"

"Gypsy." Her breath reeked of alcohol and cigarettes.

"What are you doing here, Gypsy?"

"You know what I'm doing here."

"Where do you live?"

She smiled. "Fifty bucks and when I'm done you'll beg me to do it again. Just come over here with me." She took Robin by the elbow.

"Who do you work for?" Robin asked. "I won't hurt you. I'm a reporter. I'd like to hear your story."

Gypsy studied her face. "A reporter? Get away from me." She let go of Robin's arm and hurried off down the row of semitrucks.

Philip and Carrie joined Robin as she watched Gypsy disappear. "You gave her a bus ticket?"

"Didn't do much good," Carrie said.

Philip spotted a dark-haired woman watching them from the end of the row. "We better get out of here before the muscle shows up."

They hustled back to the Highlander. Philip turned left out of the truck stop parking lot. "Anyone following us?"

Carrie twisted around in her seat to look out the back. "No."

They drove back across town to Robin's house. The traffic was sparse, and the traffic lights were synchronized, so they made good time.

"What did you think?" Carrie asked.

"I was too far away from the other women to tell much, but the girl I spoke with was a mess. She'd been beaten and she was definitely underage."

"But did you get enough for a story?" Philip asked.

"Yes, I'll have enough, I think, after I do some background research to set tonight's reporting in context. Assuming the pictures turn out."

"When will the story be in the paper?" Carrie asked.

"I'll have to run it by my editor, but that shouldn't be a problem. So maybe in the next few days, depending on breaking news."

They pulled into her driveway. The outside lights were still on. Carrie turned around in her seat. "Do you want us to go in with you?"

Robin shook her head. "No. I'm fine. I set the alarm system."

"So," Philip asked, "do you have anything for us?"

Robin hesitated for a moment. "Are we going to trade info going forward?"

"Trading off the record?" Philip asked.

"Off the record."

"Yeah, we'll trade."

"I'm working on a story about the surge in drug addiction in Cornwell. I think Pollock is operating a pill mill out of his office. I've been trying to interview his patients. Some say they buy their meds directly from him. But now, after the other night, I think Pollock must be connected with the local dealer."

"Who's he?"

"A guy named Dylan Anderson. He keeps a low profile, owns an autobody shop. Never been arrested. That's all I know right now."

"Thanks," Carrie said.

"I'm expecting you to share what you find out," Robin replied.

Robin got out of the SUV and walked up the sidewalk to her house. Philip and Carrie drove away. As she reached her front door, she heard a car door slam. She looked over her shoulder and saw a man crossing the street in the dark. She shoved her key into the deadbolt.

"Robin."

She took another look. It was Joel. She turned and waited for him. "Christ, Joel, you scared me. How long have you been waiting?"

"Just wanted to make sure you were safe. Who were those people who dropped you off?"

"Sources."

"Where've you been?"

"Working on a story."

"The Pollock story?"

"No. Did you know about the underage prostitution going on at the Paradise Truck Plaza?"

"We're always busting working girls out there."

"This looks more like sex trafficking. I talked with a girl who was banged up, high, couldn't have been more that sixteen."

"You going to stir up another hornet's nest? You need to keep your head down until we figure out who tried to kill you."

"I'm just doing my job."

"How about a nice feature on the homeless shelter?"

"Good night, Detective."

Marcos took a .38 snub-nose revolver out of his jacket pocket. "Do you know how to use this?"

"I don't need a gun."

"That isn't what I asked you."

"Yeah, I know how to use it. I used to go hunting with my dad."

"Then you take it."

"I don't need it."

"But I need for you to have it. So do me a favor."

"Okay." She took the revolver. It felt heavy in her hand.

"Take care of yourself."

"I will."

He put his hands on her hips and kissed her. "I mean it."

"I will."

Robin watched Joel walk off across her lawn into the dark. She wouldn't have described their relationship as serious. Just fun times. She slipped the revolver into her jacket pocket. He'd never been protective before. And that was how it needed to be. If he were protective, the other cops would think she wasn't able to take care of herself. She couldn't have that. She opened her front door. But now? It did feel good knowing he was watching over her. Was this his way of telling her that he really cared about her? Maybe she was in over her head on this story.

She turned on the lights, locked the door, and reset the alarm system. Why had she trusted Carrie and Philip? Because Carrie had saved her life? Or because they'd tried to help Gypsy? They were criminals, on the prowl, looking to do dirt. They didn't deny it. Would anything they told her be reliable? She needed to take a deep breath, reassess, be absolutely sure that every action she took made sense. She couldn't afford to take any unnecessary risks.

. . .

MEANWHILE, Philip and Carrie turned left off Sweetwater Boulevard onto Mall Drive. The Makepeace Valley Shopping Mall was on their right. A few stray cars were scattered around the empty parking lot. On their left were a number of small stores and offices, all closed, their fronts protected by security lights. The Wendy's was still lit up.

"Drive-through's open," Carrie said, "but the parking lot is empty and there're no cars in line."

Just beyond the Wendy's, they could see the Jones Brothers Realty and Gentle Touch Dental.

"Wish we hadn't bumped into that girl at the truck stop," Carrie said.

"She didn't see us."

"But what about the woman you saw watching us?"

"We don't know if she's with the slavers. And even if she is, we don't know if she recognized us."

"I just don't want the kid to get in any more trouble."

"Slavers are definitely going to be pissed off when the newspaper article comes out."

"Maybe we should have found a different story for Robin," Carrie said.

"Too late now. We did what we could to manage the risk."

Carrie scanned the parking lots surrounding the dental office. "All clear."

Philip pulled around to the service entrance at the back of the office. "Cameras?"

"Can't see any."

"You researched this office?"

She nodded. "They had a break-in four years ago. Nobody caught."

"So they probably did a security upgrade."

"Insurance would probably require it."

"Let's see what we've got," Philip replied.

They put on ski masks and throwaway gloves before they got out of the SUV and approached the back door. "Think there's a steel bar locked across on the other side?" Carrie asked.

"This is an emergency exit. Besides, there wouldn't be an anti-jimmy plate if the door was barred inside."

To their right, a mass of cabling came down the wall and entered the building about three feet off the ground. "Here's the phone and internet," Philip said. "So we enter. Motion alarm goes off. Security company calls Pollock at home. He tells them to call the cops. We've got how long?"

"I'd say five to ten minutes, depending on where the nearest patrol car is," Carrie replied. "I doubt if there's any security still inside the mall this late, but even if there is, they won't cross the road."

"Where do you think the safe is?"

"An office this size? It's going to be behind the receptionist's counter."

"I agree. Okay, I'm setting my timer for five minutes."

He picked the lock on the door. The bolt slid back. They turned on the flashlights on their phones and made their way down the dark hall past the patient treatment rooms to the receptionist area. Carrie looked out the front windows. All clear. Philip opened and closed the cabinets and cupboards surrounding the receptionist's station. No safe. He looked at his phone. Two minutes left.

The file cabinet beside the computer station was on wheels. He pulled it out. Bingo. The safe was built into the floor. It was the best safe in its price range, but once again, Pollock hadn't bothered to change the manufacturer's try-out combination. Inside were gallon-size plastic bags bulging with what looked like OxyContin pills and several bundles of money wrapped with rubber bands. He put the money and the drugs back in the safe, closed it, and rolled the file cabinet back into place.

He motioned to Carrie. They rushed down the hall and out the back, where he relocked the door. Sirens sounded in the distance from Sweetwater Boulevard. They hurried into their SUV. Philip turned left onto Mall Drive and sped half a block before he turned on the headlights.

Carrie twisted around in the passenger's seat, scanning the street behind them. "Still no cops."

Philip turned right into the adjoining neighborhood of apartment buildings and slowed down to the speed limit. No one was on the street and the apartments were dark inside.

"Had he changed the combination this time?" she asked.

"Bet he doesn't even know how."

"What was in the safe?"

"Pills and money."

"So Robin's right," she said.

"Yeah. But that was a lot of pills. Business must be very good. And as clueless as Pollock is, he can't possibly be on his own."

"So we've got to stay on Pollock until he meets his partners. Maybe it's this Anderson guy, maybe it's someone else. We track his connection, and we'll find out who we're up against."

He nodded.

"And you left everything in the safe exactly as you found it?"

"When Pollock and the cops get there, they'll find the doors locked and nothing taken."

THIRTY MINUTES LATER, Pollock was standing beside his BMW in the parking lot of his dental practice. The night was eerily quiet, the stars hidden by clouds. Maybe it would rain before morning. The police cruiser had been pulled up to the front door when he got there, its lights flashing, two officers walking the perimeter with their heavy flashlights. All the doors were locked. He'd opened the front door, turned off the alarm, and the cops had swept the building. Nothing had been taken or damaged. After the police left, he'd checked the safe. The pills and the money were still there. He was supposed to call the police if he noticed anything else in the morning, but right now it looked like an alarm malfunction. He'd have to call the security company tomorrow. Have them come check the system. What a waste of time. He wondered how long it would take him to get back to sleep.

5

CHASING LEADS

Over the next few days, Philip and Carrie shadowed Pollock wherever he went. They followed him from his house to his dental office to lunch, on various innocent errands, and back home, but he never met with anyone of interest. Then, on the third day, while they were sitting in the parking lot of a drycleaners with a good view of the Gentle Touch parking lot, they noticed a red Camry was also watching Pollock's office.

Carrie handed Philip the binoculars. "What do you think?"

Philip adjusted the binoculars. He saw a pudgy Asian and a white guy with a 1980s mustache. "They think they're hiding in that Camry. They're not the FBI. Not the state police. Got to be local."

"Spillage from the attack on Robin?"

"Makes sense. She's the crime reporter. She must have cop friends. And your friends are not going to believe a phony suicide. Especially when they got tipped on their hotline and ignored it."

He looked back through the binoculars. "Here we go. They're taking pictures of people coming and going from the office."

"Following in Robin's tracks."

"Exactly."

. . .

THE NEXT MORNING the truck stop prostitution story appeared below the fold on the front page of the *Herald.* The title read *Child sex trafficking at Paradise Truck Plaza.* That evening, the police raided the truck stop. A dozen officers rushed down among the parked semi-trucks, snatching up any prostitutes in the parking lot and banging on truck cab doors asking for permission to search. Several women were arrested. The rest scattered.

Carlos and Sergei drove around in the Suburban, collecting their girls who hadn't been arrested, and taking them back to the two-story clapboard house on Stafford Circle where Lincoln was waiting. By 2:00 a.m., everyone was accounted for and the remaining girls were in their rooms. Downstairs, Lincoln, Carlos, Sergei, and Daisy, an older woman with dyed black hair who managed the girls' personal needs, were gathered in the first floor room that Lincoln used for an office.

"Three of our girls are in jail," Lincoln said. "Something's not right. We've never had trouble out at the truck stop before. Not like this."

"It would have been worse if we hadn't paid off the cops," Sergei said.

"It was that newspaper article," Carlos said. "Our cop friends say that the mayor was leaning hard on the chief of police."

"Why was that reporter nosing around?" Lincoln asked.

Daisy spoke up. "I saw her talking to Gypsy. Then after Gypsy ran, those two from the other night showed up."

"The two who bought the bus ticket?"

She nodded.

Lincoln turned to Carlos. "Bring Gypsy down to the kitchen."

Lincoln, Daisy, and Sergei were seated around the Formica table in the kitchen when Carlos dragged Gypsy into the room, his hand gripping her wrist.

"Sit down," Lincoln said.

She looked from Lincoln to Daisy to Sergei, saw their cold expressions, and tried to pull away. "I didn't do anything."

"Then you've got nothing to worry about. Sit down."

She sat in the open chair next to Lincoln, Carlos standing behind her.

"The reporter talk to you?"

"I was just trying to do my job—when she said she was a reporter, I ran."

"I bet you did."

"I did. You've got to believe me."

"I believe you. The man and woman from the other night, what do you know about them?"

"Just what I told you before. They gave me a bus ticket. That's all I know."

"You don't know why they'd bring a reporter out to the truck stop?"

She shook her head. "I didn't see them with the reporter. Honest. I would have told you."

Lincoln patted her hand. "I know. I know you're a good girl, the kind of girl who learns her lesson. I know you didn't want Patty or the others to get busted. You've got nothing to be afraid of." He turned to Carlos. "Give her some dope."

AT 7:00 A.M., Davy and Sons trash haulers found Gypsy in one of their dumpsters behind a mom and pop grocery downtown. Because it involved drugs, Marcos and Bledsoe caught the case. A slow rain was falling when they arrived on the scene. Uniformed officers had the area taped off. CSI had just pulled her out of the dumpster and laid her out on a tarp on the asphalt. Rigor mortis had set in, and her face was discolored red and blue.

"What have we got, Jerry?" Marcos asked.

Jerry Gordon, a skinny black man wearing white coveralls, was squatting beside the body. "She didn't die here. Probably an OD. Young girl. Some old bruises, but nothing fresh."

"What about the face?"

"Blood pooling. She was head down."

"So she's been here awhile."

"I'm guessing someone moved her as soon as they found her dead," Gordon replied.

Bledsoe frowned. "She looks like she should have been caught in that raid last night."

Marcos nodded. "If she had been, she'd probably still be alive."

"Is there even a crime here other than dumping the body?" Bledsoe asked.

"We'll know more when we get her to the lab," Gordon replied.

Marcos got out his phone. "Hey, Robin, we found a young girl in a dumpster. She's probably a prostitute. Thought you'd want to know."

"You think it's connected to the police raid on Paradise Truck Plaza?"

"Don't know."

"But she's a kid?"

"Yeah."

"Can I get a look at her?"

"Why?"

"Because I want to know if she's the girl I talked to."

"She's headed for the morgue right now. If you want to see her, meet us there."

MARCOS WAS WAITING in the basement hallway of the Cornwell Medical Center when Robin got off the elevator. "Have you ever done this before?"

"I've seen dead bodies."

"It's not like on the TV shows."

"I know."

"Okay, then."

They walked down the hall to the morgue. He held the door for her. Bledsoe and Gordon, now wearing a lab coat over khaki pants and a striped shirt, stood next to a table where a body was covered by a sheet.

"Is this the girl?" Robin asked.

"Yes," Gordon said. "You ready? You need to get in and out before the medical examiner shows up."

She nodded.

Gordon pulled the sheet back from the girl's face. Her eyes were closed, her tangled hair smoothed back from her red-blue face, her mouth slightly ajar.

Robin felt a shiver run up her spine. She sucked in a breath, swayed, shifted her weight, and let her breath out. "That's her. That's the girl I interviewed."

"Can you tell us anything about her?" Bledsoe asked.

"She called herself Gypsy. I don't know what her real name was or anything else about her."

"That's a shame."

Robin took one last look at Gypsy's face. She looked like an extra from a zombie movie. "I'm going to find out who did this to her."

"Might just be an overdose," Bledsoe said.

"Somebody gave her the drugs," Robin replied.

"It's not your fault," Marcos said.

"Maybe it is. Maybe they did this to her because she talked to me."

"And maybe they didn't. This is a police investigation now."

"Think you'll catch them?"

"We're going to try."

Robin walked out into the hallway.

Gordon covered Gypsy's face. "Robin's really wound up."

Bledsoe turned to Marcos. "You shouldn't have promised her anything."

"I know."

"This looks like the deadest of dead ends."

"I can't disagree."

Marcos turned to Gordon. "Let us know what you find."

"Will do."

. . .

In the late afternoon, Philip and Carrie were parked at the outer edge of the Makepeace Valley Shopping Mall parking lot, watching the plainclothes cops who were parked in front of Jones Brothers Realty watching the front of the Gentle Touch Dental offices. Philip and Carrie had been here every day since they switched over from following Robin Simons, but thus far all they'd seen were dental patients and people who were likely pill purchasers.

"Think the cops are as bored as we are?" Carrie said.

"Please," Philip said, "they get paid either way. They're probably working their phones."

The pudgy Asian cop, wearing jeans and a polo shirt, got out of the Camry and walked across the street to the Wendy's. Carrie followed him with her binoculars all the way to the restaurant side door.

"Heads up," Philip said.

A white Dodge Ram pulled up to the front of the dental practice. A dark-haired man wearing slacks and dress shoes climbed out carrying a gym bag and went inside.

"It's a quarter to five," Philip said.

"So he's not a dental patient."

"Looks like the supplier."

A few minutes later he came back out carrying a manila envelope.

"Finally caught a break. What are the cops doing?"

"The other guy is still in the Wendy's."

Philip and Carrie turned out of the parking lot onto Mall Drive and fell in behind the Dodge Ram. The Ram moved leisurely through the heavy traffic on Sweetwater Boulevard, staying below the speed limit. Philip followed two cars back.

"We've been watching Pollock's office all week," Carrie said. "We didn't miss seeing the Ram before."

"No way. One of us was always there. He would have stood out."

"Which means Pollock's on the once a week re-up and pick up."

"Seems so," Philip said. "I wonder how much money is left in his safe?"

When the Ram pulled into the left turn lane at a stoplight,

Philip pulled in right behind him. After they turned onto Beaverdale Road, the traffic thinned out and Philip fell back half a block. Six blocks later, the Ram turned onto Michelle Trail, and rolled past a heating and cooling business, a cardboard box manufacturer, and a plumbing supplier, before turning into the A-Okay autobody shop.

Philip parked on the shoulder of the road outside the razor-wire-topped fence. Out in front of the building, two men wearing expensive casual clothes stood talking. One of them waved at the man driving the Ram truck. The truck disappeared into the third garage bay.

"Those guys are muscle. This must be Anderson's shop," Carrie said.

Philip nodded. "Can't be two gangsters operating out of an autobody shop in a town this size."

A tow truck pulling a Volvo sedan came through the gate and stopped at the far side of the parking lot where several banged-up cars sat in a row. A man in a ball cap and gray coveralls climbed out of the tow truck and unhooked the Volvo. "That's an actual A-Okay employee," Philip said.

"And here comes a satisfied customer," Carrie replied. A woman in a skirt and a blazer came out of the building with a man wearing work pants and a polo shirt with a logo on the chest. They stopped in front of a shiny Toyota Avalon, the woman nodding and smiling.

"Time for us to move along," Philip said. "We'll come back later for a better look."

Philip pulled back onto Michelle Trail and continued down to the four-way stop at Griffith Street, where he took a right into town. "I'm getting hungry."

"What kind of food do you want?"

"What kind do you want?"

"How about Indian?"

Carrie's burner phone rang. "Who is it?" Philip asked.

"It's the reporter." She put the phone on speaker.

"Hey, Robin. You're on speaker. We're both here."

"Gypsy is dead. Drug overdose. They found her in a dumpster this morning."

"Sorry to hear it," Philip replied. "But why are we talking?"

"You know how these traffickers think, what they'll do next. I want you to point them out to me."

"You've got a real taste for danger."

"Something has to be done."

"Why? All you can do is harass them. You've got no proof they killed the girl, and you're not going to get any."

"Maybe I can get one of the other girls to help me."

"We should have let you die the first time. It would have been a mercy. But if you insist on being crazy, they're probably working downtown at the convention center."

"Will you show me?"

"It's too early now. We'll meet you at ten o'clock."

"Where?"

"Across the street from the main entrance."

Robin hung up. Carrie put her burner phone back in her shoulder bag. "That kid is probably dead because of us. We should have left her alone."

"Maybe. But we didn't make her get in the car. And we didn't kill her. That's on the slavers."

"Well, there's nothing we can do about it now."

"Not now there isn't."

"Philip, as long as degenerates want to sleep with underage girls, somebody's going to be selling them. She wasn't one of us. Maybe we just have to let this one go."

"Maybe."

AT 10:00 P.M., Robin spotted Philip and Carrie on the corner opposite the convention center. The sidewalks were full of people streaming out of the Cirque du Soleil show and heading off toward the parking structure.

"Right on time," Philip said.

"You sure you're ready for this?" Carrie asked. "You can always change your mind."

"I'm not backing out," Robin said.

"Got a question for you first," Philip said.

"What is it?"

"Have you got anything new on Pollock?"

Robin shook her head. "Nothing. Wish I did."

"Did you know the cops have his office under surveillance?"

"Really? Are you sure?"

"Oh yeah, we're sure. You can look for yourself. They're there all day."

"I will." Robin looked from Philip to Carrie. "Let's get on with this. Where do we find the prostitutes?"

"The girls are not out in front," Carrie said. "The cops can't allow that. They're around the edges of the action. Come on."

They walked down the block toward a Hilton hotel. "See those two girls in the party dresses standing at the corner to the alley, acting like they're waiting for a ride?"

"Are you sure?"

They walked down to where they could see down the alley. "See the guy back there by the service door? He's the muscle."

"We didn't see that at the truck stop."

"They were around, but they don't have to be out in the open like they do here on the street."

"Are they with the traffickers?"

"Who knows? You'll have to talk to them to find out. You're looking for new girls, girls who weren't here a few days ago," Carrie said.

"Got you."

"Good luck," Philip added.

Philip and Carrie walked away. Robin studied the women on the corner. Several men walked by, headed for the hotel, but the women just stood there talking. Then a man walked by on his own, and one of the women stepped toward him, smiling and gesturing. The man shook his head. Now was her chance to catch them alone. As she stepped off the curb, Joel Marcos pulled up in his Dodge. The passenger window lowered. "Get in," he said.

"Are you following me?"

"Someone tried to kill you, remember?"

"I'm working."

"I can see that. Were those the same two sources you were out with the other night?"

She didn't reply.

"I'm not leaving you here."

"You're a pain in the ass."

"Get in the car."

PEANUT FRAZIER WAS STANDING in the shadows half a block back, watching Robin Simons as she talked with the black man in the car. She obviously knew him, and he was obviously a cop. First she met that man and woman in front of the convention center, and now this guy pulls up as soon as she's alone. Why couldn't she have died the first time? Tonight should have been easy. He should have been able to follow her out from the newspaper, bundle her into his car, and toss her off the 12th Street bridge into the traffic below. Instead, she kept bumping into people. He watched her get into the car. He'd have to find another way.

"WHERE'RE ARE YOU PARKED?" Marcos asked.

"At the newspaper," Robin replied.

"I'm taking you to your car and following you home."

Robin shifted in her seat and crossed her arms. "How long do you plan on doing this?"

"As long as it takes."

"Don't expect to get invited in."

Marcos took the next left to come around the block and head back toward the Herald building.

Robin sat back in her seat, looking out the window to see if she could notice where any other prostitutes were gathered. "Have you found out anything about Gypsy?"

"Not yet, but we haven't had much time to look into it. There's no evidence of foul play. She could have been left there by a drug buddy. Maybe someone will come forward when they start missing her."

"That's not very reassuring."

"We're doing the best we can."

"Is that why you're watching Pollock's office?"

"You said you had sources who'd bought drugs from Pollock. With the drugs problem as bad as it is, that was enough for the captain to authorize the surveillance. Maybe we'll see something that will lead to an arrest."

"You told the captain?"

"Steve was standing right there when you told me, remember? Everything you said went into our report."

"That was my lead. If you make an arrest, you have to call me first."

"I'll call you."

"No bullshit, Joel. I'm not kidding."

He turned into the Herald parking lot and stopped beside her Camry. "I know this isn't fair, but it's for your own good."

"I'll decide what's for my own good."

"You're going home."

She slammed his car door and got into her own car. He followed her out of the lot.

Daisy was standing on the other side of the entry to the Hilton with two of Lincoln's girls. She stuck up her hand when she saw the Suburban. It pulled up beside her and the passenger's window lowered. Lincoln looked at her expectantly. "I saw the reporter," she said. "Cop picked her up."

"You sure he was a cop?"

"There's no hiding them."

"Christ. So she's still nosing around. Did she know who you were?"

"No."

"But she's gone now?"

Daisy nodded.

Lincoln turned to Carlos. "Drive."

Carlos pulled back into traffic. "What do you want to do?"

"We're bleeding cash and we can't bail out the underage girls. That reporter is a pain in my balls. But killing her will only make trouble with the cops. Fucking grifters brought this on us. The reporter was no problem before they showed up. We found them at a motel before. So we're going to corral the girls and spread our people around, find out where they're staying, and kill them. Maybe the reporter will take a hint."

ROBIN PULLED into her garage and lowered the door before she got out of the car. She took out her smartphone, clicked on her house alarm app, and turned it off. Not arming the alarm during the day had been a mistake. That's how that guy had gotten in. She grabbed the golf club she'd left leaning beside the door to the kitchen. She knew no one could be in the house—the alarm would have kicked over—but being attacked in her own home was still raw in her mind. That guy had been waiting for her. He'd tossed her around like she was a rag doll. He could have raped her after he drugged her, and there was nothing she could have done. She reached into the kitchen and flipped on the light before she stepped into the room, golf club out in front of her like a sword. The pantry was empty. The living room, the hall, the spare bedroom—all empty. No one hiding behind the shower curtain in either bathroom. She pushed her bedroom door all the way open. Empty. She kicked off her shoes and leaned the golf club against the wall by the door. Then she went back down the hall to the alarm keypad and set the perimeter alarm. She was all alone and locked in tight.

She poured herself a glass of white wine, went to the front

window, and peeked through the curtain. The world seemed dark and quiet and safe. Was Joel still out there? God damn him, thinking he could tell her what to do. She padded back down the hall to her bedroom, changed into cotton pajamas, and then went into the bathroom, where she washed her face. Chasing down leads on Gypsy's death was going to require a lot of legwork, and a dead prostitute wasn't really news unless she'd been murdered. Sad, but that's the way it was. Maybe Philip and Carrie were right. Maybe it wasn't possible to find out who was responsible.

She carried her drink into the kitchen and looked out the back window. All clear. Like someone couldn't come through the backyard after she turned away. She needed to stop being so paranoid. The alarm would protect her. She opened her laptop on the kitchen island, went to her blog, and wrote a short piece about prostitution downtown. By the time she'd finished the blog post, her wine glass was empty. She put the glass in the sink before she went back to the bathroom and started brushing her teeth. Gypsy deserved justice. The truth needed to come out. And if the truth came out, the police would have to do something. She rinsed out her mouth and put her toothbrush away.

The .38 revolver sat on the bedside table next to her bed. She felt safer having it, but she shouldn't have accepted it. She didn't think she could shoot anyone. Besides, taking the gun shifted her relationship with Joel. Took them off their equal footing. He gave her the gun and then he showed up to protect her, his judgment trumping hers. That wasn't going to work. She climbed into bed. What did she want? She didn't want to end it if she didn't have to. They were good together, thought about the world the same way, did similar sorts of work, and the sex was great. Maybe this new protectiveness signaled that he wanted to take things to the next level. Was she ready for that? Only if he could back off. She pulled her blankets up around her shoulders. Maybe the AC was set a little low. She drifted off the sleep.

The perimeter alarm shrieked. Robin's eyes snapped open. She rolled off the mattress, grabbed her phone and the .38 from the night table, and crawled under the bed, her eyes locked on her bedroom door. The alarm cycled over and over. Her phone rang. It was her security company. She put her phone to one ear and her finger in the other ear. Before the person on the other end of the line could say anything, she said, "Break-in. Send the police. I'm hiding in my bedroom."

"Ma'am?"

"Send the police."

She ended the call and used the app on her phone to turn off the alarm. The house was still. No footsteps, no voices. She looked at her phone for the time: 2:15 a.m. Her heart was racing. She tried to slow her breathing. It seemed like forever before her phone rang again.

"Ma'am? The police are outside your home. There's no forced entry. They want you to open the door."

"Okay."

She crawled out from under the bed and walked through the house in the dark, the phone up to her ear and the gun in her other hand. She looked through the peephole in the door. Two uniformed police officers stood on her steps, an older man and a younger one. "I see the police," she said.

"Yes, ma'am."

"Thanks for your help."

She ended the call, turned on the lights, laid the gun down on the coffee table, and opened the door.

"Did you call about a break-in, ma'am?" the older officer asked.

"The alarm went off."

"Can we come in?"

"Yes."

They both came into the living room, glanced around, saw the gun on the coffee table. The older officer continued. "Could I see some ID, ma'am? For my report."

"Just a minute." Robin went back into her bedroom, put on her robe, and got her driver's license from her handbag.

"Robin Simons. You're the *Herald* reporter?"

She nodded.

"Didn't you have some trouble over here the other night?"

"Yes."

"What happened tonight?"

"I was asleep. The alarm went off. Because of the trouble last week, I just thought it was better to be safe than sorry."

"Yes, ma'am. Do you want us to look through the house?"

"No one came in."

"We didn't see anyone when we got here, and we searched around the outside."

"They must have run when the alarm went off."

"So you're okay now?"

"Yes."

"You don't want us to search inside?"

"No."

"Okay then, you give us a call if there's any more trouble."

"Thank you, officer."

"And you might want to get your alarm checked out tomorrow, just to make sure it's working properly."

"My alarm?"

"Yes, ma'am. I'm not saying you didn't have someone try to break in, but sometimes it's just the alarm, so it's always good to get it checked out."

Robin watched them get back in their cruiser before she locked the door and reset the alarm. They didn't really believe someone had tried to break in. They thought she was overreacting. What kind of rumors were floating around the police department? Did they think she had a drug problem? Did they think she was just trying to cover up a drug overdose? Make the fake intruder seem real? She picked up the .38 from the coffee table. Whoever had tried her door wouldn't be back tonight, so she was safe for now. And maybe it was just coincidence. Maybe this attempted break-in had nothing to do with that guy trying to murder her. There was no way to know.

She left the lights on in the living room, left her bedroom door open, and made sure the gun was in easy reach before she got back in bed. Pollock had hired someone to kill her. That was so hard to get her mind around. It didn't seem believable. And yet, here she was, lying in bed next to a gun she didn't want to use. Like she was in some sort of alternate reality. First attempt almost got her. If Carrie hadn't showed up, she would have died. She couldn't take any chances. She had to assume tonight wasn't a coincidence, that Pollock or whoever was going to keep trying. Well, she wasn't going to give up on the investigation. She was going to keep probing, find out where Pollock was getting his pills, expose the drug trade. Put the cops on all of them. That was the only way she'd get the killer off her back.

MEANWHILE, Philip and Carrie were sitting in their Highlander on the street across from the A-Okay autobody shop. The razor-wire-topped gate was locked up for the night, but the lights shined through the windows of the body shop, and two men wearing casual clothes sat in lawn chairs outside the door to the offices.

"No one works overnight at a body shop," Philip said. "This has got to be the stash house."

"But how big is this operation? And do they keep the cash here?"

"Good questions. We aren't going to get in there tonight. Let's come back in the early morning and see how their day develops."

At 7:00 a.m., they parked across the street from the body shop in a freshly stolen Ford F-150. The chain-link gate was now open, but the two guys sitting out the night before were still there, smoking cigarettes and drinking coffee. The morning shift started to arrive at seven thirty—guys in auto-body tech uniforms and guys in business casual clothes. The two guys sitting out front were replaced by two new guys. In total, they counted five men in business casual switching out.

"Bet if we hang around here we could follow one of these guys delivering drugs," Philip said.

"Pollock is beginning to look like a cog in the machine."

"Yes indeed, but let's go back to Pollock's office this afternoon just to make sure we didn't miss anything."

Carrie yawned. "Are we done here? Let's go get some breakfast."

Philip started the Ford. "Let's put this truck back first."

6

TRACKING TROUBLE

Across town, Robin was sitting at her kitchen island drinking her third cup of coffee, trying to clear the fog from her brain. She had gotten up early after tossing and turning the rest of the night. It seemed like a bad dream. The alarm had kicked over. The police had come. Nothing had happened. Had she really just overreacted? She looked at her phone. She had a text from her editor. What did he want? She called him.

"Good morning, Tim."

"Good morning, Robin. I didn't wake you, did I?"

"No, I've been up for a while."

"Where are you on the pill mill story?"

"I'm still trying to find a patient of Pollock's who'll make an on-the-record statement."

"Maybe you need to try a different angle."

"I'm open to suggestion."

"Heard you had another incident last night."

"My alarm went off. I called the cops. They didn't find anyone."

"I know I didn't take the first break-in as seriously as I might have, but now it looks like someone really is coming after you. Pollock's associates must think you're finding out too much."

"I wish I knew as much as they think I know."

"I noticed you dropped another prostitution piece on your blog. The prostitution story was solid, but I can't have you losing focus. We need the pill mill story."

"I'm working as fast as I can. Using all my resources. Nobody wants this story more than me."

"That's what I want to hear. Be careful but be aggressive. We need this story."

She poured the rest of her coffee down the sink and rinsed the cup. She was at a dead end. She had to get one of Pollock's patients to go on the record. There was no other way to implicate him unless the police found something, and she couldn't count on that. Her phone rang. It was Joel. "Hey."

"You okay?"

"Yes. I'm fine. They didn't get in."

"You sure you're okay?"

"Yes. The cops thought I should get my alarm checked."

"I want to see you."

"How about lunch? I could meet you at Trinity's."

"I'll see you there."

LATER THAT MORNING at A-Okay Autobody, Anderson looked up from the paperwork on his desk when Peanut Frazier lumbered into his office. "Sit down."

"Listen, Dylan—"

"Shut up. Travis told me about last night's fiasco. I'm beginning to believe you're not very good at your job."

"I was trailing her downtown last night. Thought I would catch her in an alley. Throw her off a bridge. But then she met a man and a woman near the convention center. I kept after them. When they left, I thought I had her dead to rights, but then this detective shows up, gives her a ride. So I was left with hitting the house. Didn't know there was an alarm."

"No more excuses."

Frazier stood up. "I'll get it done."

"Hold up a second," Anderson said. "The man and woman she met—were they friends?"

"I don't think so. Looked like they were showing her around."

"Sources? Or colleagues?"

Frazier shrugged.

"Let me know if you see them again. The last thing we need is more reporters."

Frazier shuffled out of the room. Anderson got out a throwaway cellphone and dialed Pollock. The phone kicked over to voice mail. "Call me."

A few minutes later, Pollock returned his call. "Dylan, sorry I couldn't answer. I was doing a procedure."

"You know that thing we've been talking about?"

"Yes."

"You're not doing anything extra until it's settled."

"Nothing but regular patients?"

"Exactly. I'll tell you when."

"Okay."

At lunchtime, Robin met Joel at the Trinity Café, a sandwich shop down the block from the *Cornwell Herald* offices. He was already seated at a table near the back, well away from the front counter and the cash register, when she arrived.

"How's your day so far?" he asked.

"I'm dragging. Didn't sleep much after the attempted break-in."

"I talked to the cops who came to your house last night. Nothing there."

Their server, a young, bearded man wearing jeans and a rainbow striped T-shirt, brought water and took their orders.

"Anyway, they're going to be circling by your house more often than usual."

"They think it's a waste of time."

"I hope they're right."

Robin glanced toward the front door. "Tim just came in. Act like I'm pumping you for info."

Joel put on an exasperated face. "Like he doesn't know we're involved?"

"He hasn't said anything about conflict of interest."

"That's because he thinks you're using me as a source."

Their server brought their sandwiches and drinks. Joel pulled the toothpick out of his BLT. "By the way, I got a call from Jerry. Bloodwork on your dead girl came back. She was full of the same counterfeit OxyContin we're been finding all over town."

"But that doesn't tell us if she was murdered or OD'd."

"No. And we'll probably never know." He took a sip of iced tea. "Did I tell you about the pills we found on your kitchen floor? I keep on forgetting."

She shook her head.

"The analysis also came back on those. They're more of the same."

"The same as Gypsy?"

"The same as everywhere. Which makes me wonder—"

"If the pills Pollock is selling are the same counterfeits."

"Exactly. That would tie him to Anderson."

"I need to get one of his patients to give me one."

"It wouldn't stand up in court. Chain of custody."

"No, but circumstantially it would be another link. And I could use the info in my story." She took a drink of iced tea and then looked off across the room before she continued. "I've got to say, Joel, that I don't know what I'm going to do about you."

"I was wondering when you were going to bring this up."

"But you were hoping I wouldn't."

"You think I'm coming on too strong."

"I think you're interfering in my work."

"I can understand why you think that."

"Look, Joel. We're good together. Our careers are complementary. And I know you have feelings for me."

"I do."

"I love you, okay? I'm just going to say it. But things aren't going to work out if you're going to be overprotective."

"I get that."

"Good."

"But you've got to give me some time to work this out. I love you, too. It's hard to see you put yourself in danger."

"I understand. I'm just used to guys trying to boss me."

He smiled. "And you're not having any of it."

"That's right."

"That's one of the things I appreciate most about you."

THAT AFTERNOON, Philip and Carrie were parked in the Makepeace Valley Shopping Mall parking lot in a stolen Subaru watching the front doors of the Gentle Touch dental practice. The same two cops in their same unmarked car were sitting in the Jones Brothers parking lot doing the same. A slow trickle of actual dental patients had been coming and going since lunch.

"Something's up," Carrie said.

"Anderson's guys probably spotted the cops," Philip said. "But let's wait it out."

At 5:00 p.m., Pollock and his staff came out of the dental practice and drove away. Philip fell in behind Pollock as he turned onto Sweetwater Boulevard. Pollock drove straight home, taking his time in the rush hour traffic, and parked in the garage. The cops were nowhere to be found. Philip turned around in a neighbor's driveway and parked on the street where they had a good view of Pollock's house. Fifteen minutes later, the daughter rode up on her bike, laid it down in the front yard next to the steps, and ran inside. A few minutes after that, the wife pulled up in the driveway in her BMW, the son jumped out of the back seat in his soccer clothes, and she continued into the garage.

"It's a waste of time following Pollock," Carrie said. "I hate to say it, because it's such a pain in the ass, but we're going to have to start trailing the couriers from the autobody shop."

"That's a car for each of us every time. And they've got to be fresh cars if we don't want to be spotted hanging out at the autobody shop."

"So that's at least two cars every day. That's a lot of cars to steal. Even if we put half of them back."

Philip pulled out onto the street. "How about if we give Billy a call? See if he's got a car connection here."

LATER THAT EVENING, Robin sat on the sofa in her living room, going through the pile of notes and photos that sat on the cushion beside her. She'd contacted twenty of Pollock's patients, and she had photos of them coming and going from Gentle Touch Dental, but she'd only managed to get three of them to give interviews, and those interviews were off the record. Pollock was selling OxyContin to his patients, but so far, she didn't have a way to prove it. She had to get someone to go on the record, someone who would give her one of the pills. If Pollock's OxyContin was the same counterfeit as the others that were floating around town, then Pollock was probably getting his from a supplier who led to Anderson, and that was just the kind of lead she needed.

The police had received an anonymous tip that someone planned to kill her. And then Carrie and Philip had warned her that Pollock was that someone. But Pollock a killer? He was a family man, sponsored a little league team, his wife was PTO president at their middle school. It didn't add up. So if it wasn't Pollock, who was it? And if it was him, why? What pushed him so far over the edge? A piece of the puzzle was missing. She had to find out what it was. With that information and the on-the-record witness, she'd be able to pressure Pollock into admitting his involvement and giving up the name of his supplier, who was probably also the person who wanted her dead. If that person was Anderson, she'd have the story of the year. Drug addiction, pill mills, organized crime.

She straightened up the pile of notes and photos and put it back into the file folder. Carrie and Philip had been following her because they were after Pollock themselves. No, that wasn't correct. They knew where Pollock was. They could do whatever they were planning to do to him whenever they wanted. So they must be looking for someone connected to Pollock, someone more important than Pollock. The pill supplier, maybe? Carrie had come into her house. But where had Philip gone? Had he followed the guy who tried to kill her when he left her house? Did they know who Pollock's pill supplier was? She picked up her phone.

"Carrie?"

"Robin. What can I do for you?"

"I need to talk."

"You're talking."

"In person."

"You're wasting your time."

"It's mine to waste."

"Hang on a second." The line was quiet for a moment. "We can meet at one o'clock tomorrow."

"How about at Dos Hermanos Mexican restaurant?"

"Where is it?"

"On Glover Street, just south of the East Valley strip mall."

"See you then."

Robin hung up her phone. What did they know and what did she have to trade? There had to be some way to get them to cooperate.

CARRIE PUT her burner phone down on her bedside table and leaned back against the pillow propped against the headboard. "Wonder what she wants."

Philip stood by the minifridge in his boxers. "Probably fishing. You want something to drink?"

"Is there any white wine left?"

He opened the fridge. "You're in luck." He poured wine into a plastic cup for her and opened a can of beer for himself before he brought the cup to her.

Her smartphone rang. It was Billy. "Hey, Billy. You're on speaker."

"I found a contact for you."

"Tell all," Philip said.

"Used car dealer. I don't know him personally, but I know a guy who vouches for him."

"What's his rate?"

"I don't know."

"But you know he's a right guy?" Carrie asked.

"Definitely. He's no snitch."

Philip glanced at Carrie. She nodded. "Give us the details."

The next morning, early, Philip and Carrie got out of their Highlander in the customer parking of Ultimate Pre-Owned Autos. The air was still cool from an overnight rain. The building was dark inside. An older man dressed in a blue blazer and khaki slacks got out of a Buick parked in front of the office. "Can I help you?"

"Bruce Adler?" Philip replied. "We talked on the phone last night."

The man glanced around the parking lot as if he expected trouble.

"You've got nothing to worry from us."

"So you need to borrow cars?"

"Sometimes more than once a day."

"What do you need them for?"

"Surveillance."

Adler nodded. "I made a call after we spoke. You're highly recommended."

"We try to be."

"This is how it works. You take a car, that's two hundred dollars. You wreck it, you've bought it. If the plate numbers are taken at a crime scene, I report it stolen. That's the deal. Take it or leave it."

"At that price, we only deal with you," Philip replied.

"And we need access to the key cabinet so that we can pick up cars on the fly," Carrie added.

"We use a computerized system," Adler said. "I'll give you a door key and you can check out the keys just like any of the salespeople. That way I'll know which cars you've taken."

. . .

An hour later, Philip and Carrie were parked in separate cars on the street in front of A-Okay Autobody, Carrie in a Ford Focus on the same side of the street as the autobody shop and Philip in a Toyota Matrix on the opposite side of the street. Water was puddled in the gutters and the air smelled of moist dirt. The two men dressed in business casual were sitting out in their lawn chairs in front of the body shop office. A tow truck rolled in, a Prius with a smashed rear end sitting up on the flatbed. Philip and Carrie were talking on their phones.

"It's already getting humid," Philip said. "It'll be horrible by lunchtime."

"How much longer do you think?"

"These guys aren't early birds, that's for sure, but you'd think they'd have to get done with their re-ups before noon."

"If they're doing that much trade."

"It's supposed to be an epidemic."

A black Jeep came out of the driveway and turned left. "I'm on him," Philip said.

Philip followed the Jeep off Michelle Trail and onto Beaverdale Road, where it pulled into a Caffeination coffee shop. The driver, a fat man wearing workout clothes with dress shoes, got out and went inside. Philip parked on the street next to the coffee shop parking lot and waited.

In the meantime, the white Dodge Ram they'd followed from Pollock's office pulled out of the A-Okay driveway and turned right, the dark-haired man behind the wheel. Carrie started after him. He made his way to Sweetwater Boulevard and headed downtown, moving through traffic as if he was in a hurry. Just to the south of the old downtown shopping district, he turned off Sweetwater onto a side street of rundown apartment buildings. A long-haired man wearing an untucked flannel shirt stood at the curb. The Dodge Ram pulled over, the man opened the passenger door and climbed in for a moment, and then got out. There was a bulge under his shirt. Carrie speed-dialed Philip. "Looks like I've got something."

"Nothing happening here."

"I'll keep you posted."

The Dodge Ram turned left at the next street, then left again to return to Sweetwater Boulevard. Several blocks later, it pulled into a parking space next to a white utility van on the west side of Veterans Memorial Park, which was located across the street from the VA Health Center. Carrie drove past them, circled through the drop-off zone in front of the health center, and parked on the other side of the street where she could watch the van. A few families and a few health center employees sat on park benches near the fountain, eating their early lunches. The dark-haired man got out of the Dodge Ram with a small duffel bag and climbed into the van. Carrie called Philip.

"My guy's making a drop to a van at the VA Health Center."

"Still nothing here."

The dark-haired man got back into the Ram.

"Got to go."

Carrie followed the Ram north on Sweetwater Boulevard. When he turned on Beaverdale Road, she kept going straight. She speed-dialed Philip again. "My guy's going back to the barn."

"Mine just ended up going home."

"Ready to meet Robin?"

"Where are you?"

"I'm on Sweetwater north of Beaverdale."

"Meet me on the corner of Sweetwater and Maple. It's a few blocks behind you. I'll park this car and ride with you."

Robin was already sitting at a table when they got to Dos Hermanos Mexican restaurant. The interior was the usual adobe and sombrero theme. Only half the tables were full, blue collar mixed with office workers, but the servers were moving as if they expected the place to fill up again. Menus and glasses of water sat at their places at the table.

"Glad you could make it," Robin said.

Philip and Carrie sat down. "The food any good here?" Philip asked.

"It's pretty decent. The entrées actually taste different from each other. I come here about once a month."

Their server came and took their orders. After he had walked away, Carrie asked, "Why did you want to see us?"

"I think you know more about Pollock than you're sharing. Who told you that Pollock wanted me dead?"

"We left you looking for working girls," Philip said. "I'm surprised you're still alive."

"Why were you there when that guy came to kill me?"

"Why do you think?"

"Because you were following me, using me to find out what you could about Pollock's activities."

"Like we told you originally," Carrie said, "somebody came after us, and we're going to make sure they aren't coming after us anymore."

"Did you know he was in my house when I went in?"

Philip shook his head. "You're in over your head. You know that, don't you?"

"Did you follow him? Do you know where he lives?"

"So what? You can't identify him."

"But you can."

"We're not going to do that."

Their server brought their plates and refilled their waters. After he walked away, Robin said, "That guy tried to break into my house the night before last."

"You don't know if it was the same guy," Carrie said.

"Does it have to be the exact same guy?"

"You're too close with the cops for our taste," Philip replied.

"What does that mean?"

"The guy in the blue Dodge Charger."

"Joel's not going to bother you."

"That's what you say. Cops always end up being cops."

"I thought we were sharing information."

"Sharing being the operative word," Philip said. "I know how we could help you, but I don't know how you could help us."

"Think about it."

"We'll talk about it later, but I can't promise you anything."

LATER THAT AFTERNOON, Philip and Carrie were parked on the side of the road outside A-Okay autobody in a Ford Fusion. The two business casual guys were sitting in their lawn chairs and an autobody tech was backing a freshly painted Honda Pilot out of a garage bay.

"This is even more boring than watching the dental office," Carrie said.

"And more dangerous. We better find our guy soon. We keep parking out here—even in new cars—and eventually they're going to spot us."

At 4:30 p.m., the black Jeep rolled into the body shop. At 5:00 p.m., the autobody techs started leaving. A few minutes later, the Dodge Ram showed up. "There's my guy," Carrie said.

"The VA re-up?"

"Yep."

Ten minutes later, a Cadillac pulled out of the body shop and turned right. The driver had a thick neck, thinning hair and wraparound sunglasses. "Likely suspect," Philip said.

They followed the Cadillac north out of town through rolling fields of soybeans interspersed with fields of corn to a development of huge houses on oversize lots surrounding a small lake. The Cadillac pulled into the driveway of a two-story colonial with thick pillars and a full balcony across the second floor. Carrie didn't bother to stop. "Finally. The boss man."

"He's definitely our target," Philip said.

"I'd like to get a look in his safe."

"The one here or the one at the shop?"

"Both."

Carrie circled the lake to get back the main road. Philip looked out over the water. An older man and a grade school age boy were fishing from a small boat. "So we know where he lives, and we know where he works. We could kill him any time. But taking his money is a different sort of problem, and we need to figure out how to do that first."

"We can't get at any safe deposit box money. We aren't set up for that," Carrie replied.

"You're right. But they're not keeping the crime money in the bank. They're selling drugs and buying drugs. That's all cash. It has to be kept somewhere where they can get their hands on it. Maybe at the body shop. But if we want to take it, we need to know more about how and when they collect it."

"It looks like they're collecting from Pollock once a week, but that might be a special arrangement," Carrie said. "And they've got to be dealing drugs from more places than that downtown street and the van at the VA. So I guess we're going to have to keep tailing them."

"Yeah, as much as I hate to risk the exposure, that's what we're going to have to do."

As they drove back into town, the traffic picked up, becoming bumper-to-bumper between Cornwell Technical College and downtown. They were stuck in the left turn lane at Johnston Drive through two cycles of the traffic light.

"You know," Carrie said, "you were pretty tough on Robin. We could have told her just a little something to string her along."

Philip shook his head. "She's too smart. I want her so hungry that when we use her, she'll snap up whatever we tell her without thinking too hard about it. So we start out with a soft no. She'll keep swimming around the hook as long as it's baited. She has to. She's got no other way to find out what she wants to know."

"What about the cop boyfriend?"

"By the time he figures out what's going on, we won't care. We'll be long gone."

Sergei strode up the steps and across the wraparound porch of the Stafford Circle house. Carlos sat in an easy chair in the living room reading a newspaper, a .45 automatic on the end table beside him. "The boss in?" Sergei asked.

Carlos nodded. Sergei walked back to Lincoln's office and knocked on the door before he went in. Lincoln didn't bother to look up from his laptop computer. "What's up?"

"I ran into the grifters."

Lincoln closed his laptop and motioned to one of the chairs facing his desk. "Where?"

"At Anderson's body shop. It was just pure luck."

"But it was them?"

"No doubt. I followed them out to Anderson's place on the lake, but then I lost them in traffic."

"Lost them in traffic? You fucking idiot."

"They'll be back."

"You sure about that?"

"They weren't hanging around there for their health, Lincoln. They're up to something."

"Pulling a job on Anderson? You think they're that crazy?"

He shrugged. "They're working something out."

"Keep an eye on the body shop. And this time, don't lose them."

THE NEXT MORNING, Philip and Carrie were back at A-Okay Autobody in a Chevy Impala and a Nissan Sentra. They followed two new guys —a black guy in a green Subaru and a skinny white guy in a Ford F-150—but neither of them made any deliveries or pickups. Carrie dropped the Sentra off at Ultimate Pre-Owned Autos and Philip picked her up in the Impala.

"This is the frustrating part," Philip said. "You don't know if you're following the wrong guys on the wrong day, or the wrong guys on the right day, or the right guys and the wrong day."

"Or if you're not even following the main pipeline," Carrie added. "We'd need at least two more people to do this right."

"Well, we're not getting two more people." He stopped at a traffic light. Pedestrians were crossing to and from the Caffeination coffee shop on the corner. "And we can't keep hanging out in front of the body shop."

"So what are we going to do?"

The light changed. "Let's get some lunch. Then we'll roll by the VA and see if the van's still there."

At 4:30 p.m., they were parked among the vehicles on the side of the road outside A-Okay Autobody. All four of the vehicles they'd followed—the Dodge Ram, the black Jeep, the green Subaru, and the Ford 5-150—drove into the A-Okay lot.

"That's all of them," Carrie said. "The Ram made two drops yesterday for sure. The guy on the street and the van at the VA. The other guys haven't done anything."

"That we know of," Philip replied.

"That we know of. Now, setting up on a guy on the street without being spotted, that's hard, and that's assuming the guy is even at the same place, but the VA van was there yesterday and today. So maybe it's a permanent feature."

"It's at a prime location. Pills on wheels for the busted-up veterans who are supposed to be tapering off."

"How about if we start watching the van tomorrow?" Carrie asked. "See who comes and goes. Maybe we can follow a courier from there."

"Sounds like a plan. Better than sitting out here in the open." He glanced over his shoulder at the street. No one was coming. "Let's get out of here."

He pulled out onto the street and drove south toward Beaverdale Road. Carrie was watching her rearview mirror. "A blue Honda pulled out after we did."

Philip turned right on Beaverdale Road, heading away from Sweetwater Boulevard. Carrie turned in her seat. "They're still behind us."

Philip pulled into the left turn lane at the next intersection, waited for a gap in the traffic and took the left on the red light. Tires squealed behind them as he sped up the block, slid through a left turn, raced down two blocks, and took another left back onto Beaverdale Road. "You see them?"

Carrie scanned the cars ahead of them. “Yeah. About a block ahead, switching lanes like they haven’t got a clue.”

“Amateurs.”

“The body shop crew?”

“Let’s find out.”

They followed the Honda into town until they were in an old neighborhood on the west side. When the Honda turned into Stafford Circle, Phillip and Carrie pulled to the curb where they had a good view. The Honda parked on the circle in front of a two-story, white clapboard house. A beefy man with a shaved head sat in a wicker chair on the wrap-around porch. Two Suburbans sat in the driveway.

“The slavers,” Philip said. “Must be where they’re keeping the girls.”

“Do you think they know where we live?”

“If they did, they wouldn’t be tailing us.”

“Wonder what they want?”

“Nothing good. I bet that newspaper story crimped their style.”

“Think they saw us downtown with Robin?”

“Don’t know, but it looks like they’re on us now.”

“What do you want to do?”

“One asshole at a time. First we hijack the drug money, kill Anderson, and expose Pollock. Once we’re even for Merlin, then we can decide what to do about these mopes.”

Back at A-Okay Autobody, Frazier sat in Anderson’s office, head down, looking at his hands. Smith stood behind him with his back against the door.

Anderson tossed a lit cigar into a heavy green ashtray. “What’s taking so long?”

“I just need a few more days. I need for her to feel a little safer so that I’ll be able to get to her.”

Anderson banged his fist on his desk. “I’m paying you to take risks so that I don’t have to take them. You should have made sure she was dead the first time. You could have killed her and gotten away before the cops arrived when the alarm kicked over. Hell, you could have shot her on the street with that couple. I'm not sure if it's stupidity or lack of guts, but I'm losing patience."

"I understand."

"I don't think you do. Every day she's working on the pill story is a day she's closer to interfering in our business."

"I'll get it done."

"By tomorrow."

"By tomorrow." Frazier stood up. "I didn't know you didn't care about collateral damage. If I'd have known I could have killed the couple—" He stopped, looked back at Smith, glanced out the window, and then turned back to Anderson.

"You got something to say?" Anderson asked.

"That couple? The couple who were with Simons at the convention center? They were parked across the street when I came in here."

"You sure?"

"Absolutely."

"Describe them."

ROBIN WAS at her desk at the *Cornwell Herald*, just getting ready to leave the office when her desk phone rang. "Simons," she said.

"Robin? This is Christa Meyers."

Robin slid a legal pad into reach and picked up a pencil. "What can I do for you, Christa?"

"I've thought about what you said, and I would like for you to tell George's story."

"Can you meet now?"

"I've got to go to work in about two hours."

"You're at home?"

"Yes."

"I'll be right there."

Robin drove west to get out of the downtown rush hour traffic as quickly as possible, and then drove north on Chestnut Street to the apartments south of the medical center. She couldn't believe her luck. When she had first contacted Christa Meyers, she'd refused to talk with her. She was still ashamed that her husband George had OD'd. The second time, she'd been willing to talk off the record. George had slipped a disc at work, had two surgeries, never got better, was in constant pain. Started buying pills on the street when the doctors stopped prescribing them. Heard about Dr. Pollock from a friend. Felt safer buying his pills there. Nothing changed until one day when she got home from work and found him dead in his recliner in the living room.

Robin pulled into the apartment complex. Christa lived in an end unit near the outdoor basketball court. A group of teenagers were hustling up and down the half court, casually fouling each other and calling out for the ball. Robin parked in a visitor's space and hurried up to Christa's door. The apartment was just as she remembered it. The living room was tidy. Two pictures sat on top of the bookshelf next to the TV, one of Christa and George on their wedding day, the other of George on a motorcycle. Christa ushered her through to the kitchen, where they sat at the table.

"Do you want some coffee?" Christa asked.

"No thank you." Robin got out her tape recorder. "Are you ready?"

Christa nodded.

"Start at the beginning."

Robin took her statement, occasionally prompting her to add details about George's relationship with Pollock's dental practice. He never got dental care there, never received a billing, always paid cash. Shortly after he died, when Christa finally got the nerve to confront Pollock about what had happened, he was firm about his lack of liability.

"He said he was sorry for my loss, but that George took too many pills and that wasn't something he had control over."

Robin nodded her head sympathetically. "Do you still have any of the pills George bought from Pollock?"

"I don't know." She slid her chair back. "I probably flushed them, but let me look."

Christa disappeared down the hallway to the bedrooms. She came back in a few minutes with an envelope that contained several OxyContin pills. "Here they are."

"Are you sure these pills are the pills that your husband bought from Gentle Touch Dental?"

She nodded.

Robin smiled. "The recorder can't see you nod."

"Yes," Christa said, "these are the pills George bought from Dr. Pollock."

"Could I have one?"

"Sure."

"Set it on the table."

Robin photographed the pill on both sides with her smartphone. She showed the photographs to Christa. "Are these photos on my phone photos of the pill you gave me?"

"Yes."

"Okay. We're all done for now. Thanks so much." Robin turned off the recording. "You're doing the right thing."

"It's still hard."

"Telling George's story is going to save someone else's life."

Robin was smiling as she walked back down the sidewalk to her car. She finally had an on-the-record statement and the human interest story. She'd show the pill and the photos to Joel and Steve before she had them test it to confirm if it was part of the counterfeit OxyContin circulating in town. If it was, it would connect Pollock to the rest of the illegal drug trade.

INSIDE THE HOUSE on Stafford Circle, Sergei sat in the living room talking with Lincoln. "I followed them from the body shop again. But they're pros. They spotted me and lost me again. I need another guy in another car, so we can work them back and forth."

"We already knew they were players. That they would ditch you shows they're planning something. Otherwise, they just would have driven to a public place and confronted you." Lincoln leaned back in his seat with his hands laced behind his head. "Anderson runs drugs. So these two have got to be after drugs or drug money. And every addict in town knows where Anderson's guys are selling from. So you and Carlos are going to shake down some junkies, find out where Anderson's spots are, and check them out until you figure out which ones the grifters are watching."

"Grab them and dump them somewhere?"

Lincoln leaned forward. "Leave them in the street for all I care. Just make sure they're dead. I don't know why they were soft on Gypsy, and I don't know why they put the reporter on us. But we need to get back in business. And without their help, I don't think the reporter'll be much trouble."

7

BOBBING AND WEAVING

The next day, Philip and Carrie sat in a Volkswagen Jetta across the street from Veterans Memorial Park. The sun was shining, the flowers were in bloom, and men and women, some dressed from their doctors' appointments, some wearing the clothes they'd been sleeping in all week, were discreetly slipping up to the white utility van parked near the walkway to the fountain, where they put their hand in the window and then walked away.

"Just like printing money," Philip said.

"A lot more cash here than at Pollock's. They must be paying the cops."

Carrie went out for coffee. Philip picked up their lunch. Medical staff came and went from the park, picnicking on the benches. Philip and Carrie counted three people in the van, based on who went on errands, two men and a woman. No one seemed to pay the least bit of attention to the van or its customers. At 3:00 p.m., the Dodge Ram pulled into the space next to the van. The dark-haired man, neatly dressed in a button-up shirt and slacks, got out of the Ram and got into the passenger's seat of the van. A few minutes later, he left with a small duffel bag.

When he drove away, Philip and Carrie followed. He drove downtown, following the same route he'd taken the other morning. When he pulled up to a parked Saturn, a long-haired man dressed in work clothes got out and handed him a bag through his window. "That was the guy from the other morning," Carrie said.

The Ram made a U-turn at the end of the block. Philip circled around to get back behind it. The Ram drove east, into an area of mixed commercial and residential, and pulled into a strip mall anchored by a Pro Cosmetics outlet. A woman wearing a white pantsuit, her red hair loose around her shoulders, got out of a Buick just as the Ram pulled up. The Ram's driver climbed out, smiling and gesturing. She laughed, spoke for a moment, and then handed him a manila envelope. He got back in the truck and drove north, driving the speed limit in the busying traffic, and wound up back at the autobody shop before 5:00 p.m.

Philip drove past the gate. "The money comes here. But all we know about is the VA run."

"Can we hit the autobody shop overnight?"

"The lights are on. Two guys are sitting outside. The gate is locked. We don't know what's inside the building. Too many unknowns."

"Then we'll have to settle for the Dodge Ram daily cash," Carrie said.

"I hate to admit it—I'd love to raid the stash—but I think you're right. We'll have to take it on the road after the last pickup. A Dodge Ram can take a lot of push. Best spot would be the two-way stop at the underpass."

"Or when he's out of the truck at the strip mall," Carrie replied.

At Beaverdale Road, they took a left toward Maple Avenue. Carrie glanced out the back window. "I think that Ford's following us."

"Traffickers again?"

"Can't tell. They're too far back."

On Maple Avenue, he drove north toward the beltway. "They're keeping their distance," Carrie said.

He sped up, turned right into a residential neighborhood of

single-story houses that all looked the same, drove two blocks and parked on the street in front of an elementary school. A group of boys were practicing soccer on the playground. The Ford drove by them. It didn't slow down and the two men in the front seats—sunglasses and golf shirts—didn't glance over at them.

"Not the slavers, not the cops," Philip said.

"Got to be Anderson's guys," Carrie said.

Philip pulled out after them, following them to the end of the block, and then turned left after they turned right. He sped back down to Maple Avenue, slid around the corner, and pushed his way through the thickening traffic, passing at every opportunity. "They back there?"

"Half a block back."

The light at the intersection ahead of him turned yellow. The Nissan in front of him tapped its brakes. He drove over the curb onto the sidewalk, passed the Nissan, dropped onto the intersection as the light turned red, and stepped on the gas. The traffic closed in behind them.

"Lost them," Carrie said.

"We got lucky," Philip said.

"So Anderson's finally caught on to us."

"Yeah, now everything gets tricky. We can't let him spot us again."

THE FORD HURRIED down Maple Avenue all the way to the beltway interchange, but the Jetta was gone. "When did they make us?" the passenger asked.

"Dougie," the driver said, "they were on us from the start."

"Well, you've got to explain it to the boss."

"Why me?"

"Because you were driving, Tom."

"That's bullshit."

"Too bad."

When they got back to the autobody shop, Anderson was standing outside the office, talking with the shop manager. After the manager walked away, Anderson waved them over. "You're back awful quick."

Tom started in. "They're pros, boss. They spotted us from the get-go, weren't afraid to test us or to run a light."

"Peanut saw them with Simons. And they've been nosing around here. I don't believe in coincidence. You're going to reach out to all our people. Everyone's going to be looking until we find them."

It was already dark when Robin Simons came out of the Herald building and got into her car. Frazier, dressed for night work, sat in a stolen Jeep Cherokee in a metered parking place. He followed her, keeping well back, as she took her usual route to her house. He parked on the street as she pulled into her garage. The neighborhood was quiet. Lights were on in the nearby houses, but no one was on the street, no children, no dog walkers. Just parked cars. He gave her a few minutes to turn off her home alarm, then he pulled on a pair of latex gloves, checked his 9-millimeter pistol, and pulled on his ski mask. He moved quickly across her yard, almost at a run, took the steps two at a time, and kicked in her door. The door snapped back. He saw her drop the glass in her hand and run across the living room toward the hall.

He ran after her, his gun arm outstretched, glancing into the bathroom and the spare bedroom, before he found her in her bedroom, digging in her bedside table. He fired as she spun toward him, a .38 revolver in her hand. His shot caught her in the shoulder. Her shot went wild.

"Police!"

He shifted his weight, heard the shot as he felt the bullet explode through his back into his gut. He swung around, lost his balance, and fell.

Marcos moved forward; his pistol pointed at the intruder's chest. The intruder's eyes were closed, and his chest was heaving. His gun arm lay flopped out at his side. Marcos stepped on the intruder's wrist and wrenched the pistol loose.

He turned to Robin. "You okay?"

Robin was on the floor, leaning against the bedside table, blood running down her arm, the .38 still in her hand. She had an expression on her face like she couldn't believe what was happening.

"Joel?"

Marcos slipped the intruder's pistol in his jacket pocket and called in to police dispatch. Then he got down on his knees next to of Robin. "You're safe now," he said. "You can hand me the gun."

She looked at the revolver in her hand. "Didn't know I was still holding it."

"I know."

He laid the .38 revolver on the bedside table. "Ambulance is on the way. You're not bleeding too much." He pulled the pillow case off a pillow, folded it, and handed it to her. "Put pressure on the wound."

She pressed the pillowcase against her shoulder. He put two fingers on her throat. "Your pulse is steady. You're doing great."

He glanced back at the intruder. "I need to check on him." He crawled over to him, pulled off his ski mask, and pushed him up on his side. There wasn't much blood. He lowered him back down.

The room seemed unnaturally quiet. The seconds ticked off like minutes. Finally, the silence was broken by sirens in the distance that became louder and louder until they abruptly stopped, and two uniformed officers rushed into the bedroom, guns drawn. Marcos held up his badge.

"You okay?" the first officer asked.

"Yeah," Marcos replied. "Can you guys manage the outside?"

A few minutes later, two EMTs came into the bedroom carrying a gurney. The older one stopped with the intruder. Marcos moved back over toward Robin. The younger EMT knelt down beside her and checked her vital signs. "You were lucky," he said.

"More than once."

"This one's bad," the older EMT said.

"You rest," the younger EMT said to Robin. "We have to take him first."

They shifted the intruder onto the gurney, raised it, and rolled him away.

Detective Lewis hurried into the room, his hands in the pockets of his wrinkled gray suit. "Hey, Joel. Second ambulance just pulled in."

"Troy, you catch this case?" Marcos asked.

Lewis ran a hand back over his bald head and shrugged. "Luck of the draw."

Two more EMTs came in and put Robin on a gurney. "We'll talk tomorrow, Ms. Simons," Lewis said.

"I'll be at the hospital as soon as I can," Marcos said. The EMTs took Robin away.

Lewis turned to Marcos. "What were you doing here?"

"I'd come over to check on her, but she hadn't come home yet."

"So you were waiting?"

"Yeah. I'm parked across the street."

"You weren't in here already?"

"No. Saw her roll into the garage. Hadn't gotten out of my car when that guy was running across the yard."

"So you saw that guy kick the door in?"

"Yeah."

"Hell of a thing."

"I was almost too late."

"But you weren't." Lewis glanced around. "You touch anything?"

"My fingerprints are all over this place." Marcos dug the automatic pistol out of his jacket pocket. "Took this off the perp after I shot him. Might be some fingerprints on the bullets. Pulled off his ski mask to render aid."

Lewis took the pistol. Then he nodded toward the .38 revolver on the bedside table. "That one hers?"

"It's mine. I lent it to her. It's been fired. Shot went through the ceiling somewhere."

"So he kicked in the door, she was running for the .38, he shot her, she missed, and you shot him?"

"In the back. I was behind him. I identified myself and fired."

He frowned. "Anything else?"

"That's it."

"Pretty straightforward then. Why don't you get on out of here and let me do my job?"

THE NEXT MORNING, Philip and Carrie were in their motel room getting dressed for the day, drinking the thin coffee made in the in-room coffee maker, and listening to the local TV morning news, when the story about the shooting at Robin's house came on.

"Hey, honey, quick," Carrie said.

Philip poked his head out of the bathroom just as the TV was showing the outside of Robin's house.

"How much did you hear?" Carrie asked.

"Something about a shootout. Can you google it for me?"

Carrie opened her laptop computer and found the story. "Okay. Guy broke into Robin's, shot her, Detective Marcos—isn't that the boyfriend?"

"I think you're right."

"He shot the guy. Robin's in stable condition and the guy's in the ICU." She scanned the rest of the article. "Looks like Detective Boyfriend is going to get a medal."

Philip put on his sports coat. "This really works for us. It won't take long for the cops to figure out the ICU guy is one of Anderson's."

"If they don't already know."

"Then they'll be hard after Anderson, and he'll be preoccupied trying to stay out from under."

Carrie finished her coffee and tossed the Styrofoam cup into the trash. "You want to have a look in Anderson's house?"

"You read my mind. Let's get some breakfast and make a plan."

After breakfast, they stole a utility van from the fenced lot behind a cable company office and drove north of town to Anderson's lake house. At the next-door neighbor's house, five Latinos were mowing the front and placing mulch around the flower beds. Carrie parked the van next to a power pole down the street. Philip got out of the van wearing coveralls and set a ladder against the pole. Just another cable guy.

Carrie sat in the van watching Anderson's house while Philip pretended to be fixing something. A middle-age blonde backed out of the garage in a Cadillac Escalade, a grade-school girl in the back seat. In twenty minutes, the blonde was back. She left the SUV parked in the driveway and went inside. An hour later, she came out in yoga clothes and drove away. Philip climbed down from the pole, collapsed the ladder, and slid it into the rack on the top of the van. The Latinos next door were busy minding their own business. He drove the van up Anderson's driveway, and he and Carrie strolled up to the front porch, pulling on throwaway gloves as they walked. She rang the bell while he pushed his lock picks into the door lock.

"You think she set the alarm?" she asked.

"Middle of the day in a neighborhood like this? No way."

He opened the door. No siren. The wall keypad indicated that the system was unarmed. They moved through the entryway, down the hallway past the formal living room and dining room, and into the family room that faced the lake.

"No office," Philip said.

"Let's try upstairs."

They went up the stairs. Daughter's room. Master. Spare. And home office. The safe was in the wall of the closet. Philip smiled. "I bet they had this put in when they built the house."

"How tough?"

"Have a look around." Phillip pulled up the try-out combination list on his phone. No luck. He took a piece of paper and a pencil from the desk, stepped in close to the safe, spun the dial to reset the lock wheels, and then slowly turned the dial, listening for the clicks that indicated the contact points and graphing the clicks to determine the safe combination.

Carrie went down the hall to the master bedroom. King-size bed, his and hers walk-in closets, his and hers bathrooms. She went into her bathroom, dumped the trash out of the trashcan, and took the trash bag. She looked through the bathroom drawers—cosmetics, fancy soap, the usual essentials. She moved on to her closet. She found the jewelry in the top drawer of a built-in chest of drawers. Two diamond rings, a black pearl necklace with matching earrings, a ruby pendant, some small pieces. Not as much as she might have expected, but she took it all anyway. She crossed the room to his closet. Three high-end watches—not worth the trouble—and a gold signet ring. She dropped the ring in the bag.

When she went out into the hall, Philip was moving toward her carrying his own trash bag.

"What did you find?"

"Seventy thousand in hundreds. Most of the cash must be somewhere else. What have you got?"

"Some jewelry. Nothing special."

They went back out the front. The Latinos were still hard at work. Carrie got in the van while Philip walked around the side of the house and pretended to do something at the cable box. Then he joined her in the van and Carrie backed out of the driveway.

"He's going to be pissed when he finds out he's been robbed," Carrie said. "Think she's going to admit to not setting the alarm?"

Philip chuckled. "His trouble is just starting. We're going to multiply his problems until he can't think straight, and then we're going to kill him."

ANDERSON SAT in his office at A-Okay Autobody, a half cup of cold coffee in front of him, this morning's *Cornwell Herald* lying with the front page staring up at him. Travis Smith sat across the desk from him. "When did you find out about this clusterfuck?"

"Our guy at the hospital called me around three a.m."

"Don't leave out anything."

"Just like the papers say, Peanut barged into Simons's house to kill her. Shot her, but Marcos shot him."

"So the cops were waiting on him?"

"Looks that way."

"Is Simons dead?"

Smith shook his head. "She's in stable condition."

"Can Peanut talk?"

"He's unconscious."

"What are his chances?"

"Our guy says it's a roll of the dice."

"What an idiot."

"The cops know he belongs to us."

"But that's all they know. Maybe we'll get lucky and he'll die."

AT THE CORNWELL MEDICAL CENTER, Marcos sat in a plastic chair next to Robin's bed. Her room caught the morning light. The *Herald* had sent a colorful bouquet, which sat on the windowsill. She was sitting up in bed, drinking water through a straw, her left arm in a sling. The TV was turned on to a news channel with the sound on low.

"Have you gotten any sleep at all?" Robin asked.

"I got a few hours."

"You need a nap."

"I've got the day off."

"You deserve it."

"It's just so they can rule on the shooting."

"The chief was calling you a hero on TV."

"Still have to follow the rules."

"What about that guy?"

"Peanut Frazier? He's in a coma. When he wakes up, he's going to have make a deal."

"Do you know anything about him?"

"You don't ever quit trying to take advantage, do you?"

"It's my job."

"He's supposedly one of Dylan Anderson's guys."

"Supposedly?"

"You know how hard it is to get any good information on what Anderson is up to."

"So Anderson's the guy who's been trying to kill me?"

"Maybe. We'll find out when Frazier wakes up."

Robin turned off the TV. "Can you help me get out of here? I need to get back to work on my story."

Marcos shook his head. "You're still heavily medicated."

"Look. This story's going to blow up. All my competition will be working on it. I'm going to lose my advantage in a hurry. Months of legwork all for nothing. If I don't get moving, Tim will ask for my notes and assign James or Stacy."

"If you leave against medical advice, your insurance won't cover whatever happens."

"Nothing is going to happen."

"I bet you can't walk to the end of the hall and back."

"Please."

"Look, you just came in here last night. Do what you're told, maybe you'll get out of here tomorrow."

She rolled her eyes. "You're not my mom."

"That's for sure. I won't stand in your way, but I'm not going to help you do anything stupid. One more day."

ANDERSON WAS WALKING through the garages at A-Okay Autobody, making the rounds, visually checking over vehicles in the process of being repaired and talking with his technicians, when he got a phone call from his wife.

"Sally, what's up?"

"I think we've been robbed."

"Robbed? Slow down."

"I can't find any of my jewelry. The drawer is empty."

"The drawer in your closet?"

"What drawer would I be talking about?"

"Calm down."

"I put my jewelry away last night. I looked just now. It's gone."

"Cleaners weren't here today?"

"No, Gloria was here yesterday. We've been robbed."

"I'm on my way."

Anderson sped through the yellow light at the intersection of Sweetwater Boulevard and Kingman Road. What a waste of time. There was no reasoning with her when she got wound up. The jewelry had to be there somewhere. But if he didn't rush out and deal with it now, she'd be calling all day.

When he pulled into the driveway, Sally came out on the porch to meet him. "Finally," she said.

"I got here as fast as I could," he replied.

They went up into the master bedroom, into her walk-in closet and over to the built-in chest of drawers. Her jewelry drawer was empty. He pulled open the other drawers, Sally watching over his shoulder.

"I already looked," she said.

Sweaters, underwear, socks, but no missing jewelry. He turned on the flashlight on his smartphone and looked under the chest. Nothing.

"Oh, hell," he said. He rushed down the hall to his office, into the closet, and input the combination on the safe. The stack of papers was still there, but all the money was gone. Peanut arrested and now this. He shut the door to the safe and met Sally in the hall.

"The safe?" she asked.

"The money's gone."

"Oh my God. Somebody was in our house."

"You took Meggie to school. Where else did you go?"

"To my yoga class."

"Same trip?"

"No, I came home first."

"And you set the alarm both times?"

"I—uh—"

"Didn't set the alarm?"

"I was just gone an hour."

"We've talked about this. That's how these burglars work—walk into an empty house and take what they can."

"But the safe."

"I know. You haven't noticed anything else missing?"

"I haven't looked. Do we call the police?"

"No."

"But what about my jewelry?"

"The police won't get your jewelry back. I'll talk to some people I know. Look around the house for anything else that's missing. Let me know. I've got to get back to work."

He took his time driving back to the body shop. Who would be stupid enough to rob his house? Not anyone local. Simons should have been easy to deal with, but there she was, still alive. And the man and woman who'd been seen with her, who'd been watching the body shop, who'd outrun his guys—just who the hell were they? Not amateurs. What did they have to do with Simons? Where did they come from? Why were they helping her? Everything was going fine until Pollock bungled into that murder-for-hire scam. He banged his fist on the steering wheel. Tom and Dougie were supposed to find that couple.

THAT AFTERNOON, Philip and Carrie were following the Dodge Ram through its pickups—the VA, the downtown, and the strip mall—trailing a few cars back in a Volvo they'd taken from Ultimate Pre-Owned Autos. They were wearing gloves, Kevlar vests, and hooded sweatshirts. Their AR-15 rifles were leaning in the floorboard beside them. The plan was to shoot out the Ram's rear tires while it was stopped at the two-way stop sign on the other side of the railroad underpass, kill the driver, and take the money.

So far so good. The Ram drove away from the strip mall and was traveling the same route as yesterday. Traffic was light. The sky to the west was cloudy, hiding the sun. A school bus was stopped ahead of them, letting out children. Behind the bus was a Camry, then the Dodge Ram, then a Honda SUV, and finally their Volvo. The bus driver folded in the bus's driver's side stop sign and started moving. The Camry and the Ram passed it, but the Honda was a little too slow, so it had to wait for the oncoming traffic. Two cars came by.

Then the Honda passed the school bus just before an intersection. The light was still green. Philip and Carrie were right behind the bus. As the light turned yellow, a Ford Explorer sped through the traffic light from their right and plowed into them, pushing their Volvo through the intersection. The front quarter panel smashed into a traffic light pole. The airbags exploded. Philip shook his head, trying to understand what was happening. He turned to Carrie. She was fumbling to unlatch her seatbelt. Two men climbed out of the Explorer, pistols in their hands. Philip grabbed Carrie's shoulder and pushed her down in the seat as he raised his AR-15 and fired. The two men ducked behind their car doors.

Philip climbed out of the driver's door, firing through the Volvo's windows until he was behind the back wheel, from where he blasted away at the Explorer, keeping the two men pinned down. Carrie crawled out the driver's side behind him, her rifle in front of her, rolled onto the ground, and began firing under the car, looking for legs and feet. Philip switched out his magazine. The two guys were backing toward the rear of the Explorer. Philip stepped out from behind the Volvo. Carrie shot one of them in the ankle. As that guy hopped, Philip shot him in the chest. The second guy started to run. Philip put two rounds in his back.

Philip turned in a circle, taking in the scene. Three cars sat at the intersection. He could see phones being held up to record. "Baby," he yelled. "You good?"

"Yeah," Carrie replied.

"Let's get out of here."

He pulled the duffel containing the rest of their gear out of the back seat, and then they ran off into the neighborhood. At the end of the block they turned right, cut through a side yard and stood up against the back of a duplex, where they pulled off their vests and put the vests and the rifles into the duffel. They could hear police sirens getting louder.

"We need to find a car old enough to hotwire."

"Why? The tablet is in the gear bag."

"Really?"

"I thought we might need it."

He dug through the gear duffel until he found a small computer tablet especially designed for overriding the car computers on newer cars. "You're the best."

They walked out onto the sidewalk in front of the duplex. An old Subaru cruised past them without slowing down. As soon as it turned the corner, they walked up to the closest vehicle, a blue Nissan Sentra. Philip paired the Sentra's computer with the tablet, unlocked the doors and started the car. They drove north away from the wreck, Carrie behind the wheel, circling around to make sure they weren't being followed.

"That wasn't the drug crew," Carrie said.

"No, that was the slavers. The second one I shot was the bruiser with the Russian tattoo on his neck. Shouldn't have underestimated those pricks."

"There're two less of them."

"You're always thinking on the bright side."

Carrie turned right at the corner. "Better call Adler."

Philip put a burner phone on speaker and made the call.

"Hello?"

"You need to report the Volvo as stolen."

"Is it wrecked?"

"Total loss."

"That's going to cost you twenty-five thousand."

"A deal's a deal."

"The cops will be on me now."

"Sorry about that. You won't see us again. Might be a few days, but we'll drop your keys and the cash we owe before we leave town."

They drove back to the Best Western. There was no one suspicious in the parking lot.

"Looks safe," Philip said. "But we can't take a chance on staying here."

"How about that Budget Inn at the south interchange?"

"Sounds good."

They packed and loaded all their gear into the Highlander. Philip followed Carrie to a Walmart, where she left the Sentra in a camera blind spot.

"The traffickers are going to be up on the route."

"Yeah, we're going to have to go over our plan."

BACK AT THE WRECK, Detective Bledsoe got out of his car and walked over to the police tape. A uniformed officer held it up for him to walk under. He spotted Detective Rodriguez, a small, dark-skinned man wearing a blue suit and a brightly colored tie, standing over a body in back of a smashed Explorer. Another body lay close by.

"Hey, Mike," Bledsoe said.

"Steve, what brings you around this little war zone?"

Bledsoe peered down at the dead man. "Wondering if there was anything for the drug task force, but these don't look like any of Anderson's guys."

"Witnesses recorded the whole thing on their phones. The Explorer T-boned the Volvo, then everybody came out shooting. The man and woman in the Volvo killed these two and ran off."

"Any good pictures?"

"Assault rifles, Kevlar, hoods—can't see their faces."

"Looks like a tough nut to crack," Bledsoe said. "Any idea who these mopes belong to?"

Rodriguez shook his head. "I'll know before I'm through. I heard about Joel. How's he doing?"

"Itching to get back on the street."

"He's one fearless bastard."

"Glad he's my partner." Bledsoe took one last look around. "Well, I'll leave you to it."

"Tell Joel I asked after him."

8

WORKING THE PLAN

Philip and Carrie were sitting at the table in their motel room eating take-out Chinese and drinking beer. "Let's talk this through," Philip said. "We can't take the money en route because the slavers are on to us. But we know the daily money ends up at the body shop. And Anderson still doesn't know we're after him and the money."

"But he will as soon as he looks in his home safe or his wife misses her jewelry."

"Eventually he'll connect that to us, but maybe not at first." Philip took a drink of beer. "So the main stash is probably at the body shop, protected twenty-four seven, just like the drugs."

"That's a tough score."

"We've got to keep putting pressure on him."

"He's got his guy in the ICU to worry about," Carrie said. "Is he going to wake up and cooperate with the police?"

"Let's see if we can add Pollock to his load. And then, tomorrow, while his head is spinning, maybe we can find a way to take the daily money."

"What about the traffickers?"

"What exactly do they know? They must have been tracking us

from the VA. If we see them there, we'll deal with them before we go for the money. If we don't see them, we'll have to let the daily money go. Then all we have left is Anderson."

"What are we going to do about Pollock?"

"We know he's dirty. Let's rob him and put the police on him."

At two in the morning they drove over to Gentle Touch Dental. The area was completely quiet—no cops on stakeout, no nearby parked cars, no one in the Wendy's drive-through. They pulled around the back, just as they had before, entered the building, opened the safe, and took the money—three bundles of bills, each labeled one thousand dollars—as well as one plastic bag of OxyContin. They left three bags of pills in the open safe and the back door wide open. For good measure, Carrie called 911 on a burner phone. "I think I saw people inside Gentle Touch Dental at the Makepeace Valley Mall." She ended the call and tossed the phone out the window.

A POLICE CAR was in the front parking lot, its lights flashing, a police officer standing at the front door, when Pollock arrived at his dental office. He parked in his usual space at the end of the row. The lights were on in the office. Pollock, dressed in sweatpants and a T-shirt, got out of his car and went up to the officer. "I'm John Pollock. I got a call from my security company."

"Do you have some ID?" the officer replied.

Pollock handed the officer his driver's license. The officer used his flashlight to read it. "Dr. Pollock"—he handed the driver's license back—"you need to wait until my partner clears the building."

"Clears the building?"

"The back door was hanging open. We need to make sure no one's inside."

A moment later, a second police officer appeared on the other side of the glass door. He waved them in. "You can go in," the first officer said.

Pollock opened the front door. The first officer followed him through to the receptionist's area, where the second officer was standing. The rolling file cabinet was out of place and the floor safe was open.

Pollock looked from the officer to the safe. The pills and the money. He hoped they were gone.

"What's that in the safe?" the second officer asked.

Pollock stepped closer to look. "I don't know."

"Looks like bags of pills."

"You don't have any right to look in that safe," Pollock replied.

"The safe's open. What do you see, Goines?"

The first officer stepped around Pollock to look down into the safe. "Gallon-size bags of pills."

"I don't know what those are." Pollock said. "Or how they got there. The people who broke in must have left them there."

"I'm calling this in," the second officer said.

"I'm telling you those pills aren't mine."

Goines got out his handcuffs. "You're under arrest, sir."

THE NEXT MORNING, Pollock was sitting in an interview room at the police station wearing an orange jumpsuit and handcuffs. He hadn't slept since the officers had brought him in. Marcos came into the room with a cup of coffee in his hand. "Good morning, Dr. Pollock. Brought you some coffee." He set the coffee on the table. "Let's get those handcuffs off."

He unlocked Pollock's handcuffs and pushed the coffee closer to Pollock before he sat down. Pollock picked up the coffee and sipped it.

"Dr. Pollock, I'm Detective Joel Marcos with the drug task force. Did the officers read you your rights?"

"Yes."

"Do you understand them?"

"I'm not an illiterate. Of course I understand them."

"Good," Marcos said. "I won't lie to you. You're in a bad place."

"Those drugs aren't mine. They were planted."

"By who?"

"How would I know? I just know they're not mine."

"Last night, it was late, you might not have noticed, but the officers were wearing latex gloves. And Officer Goines was careful not to touch the outside of the plastic bags in the areas where a person might touch the bags to open them."

"I have no idea."

"They took your fingerprints when you were processed last night."

"So?"

"The lab dusted the plastic bags ASAP. Several sets of fingerprints are on the outside of the bags, including yours."

"I want my lawyer."

"Now's the time to explain yourself."

"Lawyer."

"I'll see you get your phone call."

Marcos left the room. Bledsoe was waiting in the hall. "Well?"

"He wants his lawyer. Going to let him stew a bit before he gets his phone call."

"He's screwed. He has to roll on his dealer."

"Might take him awhile to figure that out. I'll be back in a minute."

Marcos went out into the parking lot beside the police station and stood in the shade of a maple next to a picnic table. He got out his phone and called Robin's smartphone.

"You still in the hospital?"

"I go home today."

"How are you feeling?"

"Sore. Okay. Ready to get out of here."

"You still interested in Pollock?"

"Definitely."

"He's in the city jail. Last night his office was broken into. When police responded, they found the back door open and swept the building. His safe was open. Bags of OxyContin were visible."

"Has he made a deal?"

"Not yet."

"Thanks, Joel."

"You need me to drive you home?"

"No, I'm fine."

"I'll check up on you later."

PHILIP AND CARRIE pulled into the parking lot of All State Specialty Auto Parts and Police Supply. A restored cherry-red 1968 Corvette convertible with the top down sat facing the street in the corner of the lot. Two work trucks and a blue utility van were parked near the door.

"This looks like the place," Philip said. "Wait here."

Philip got out of the Highlander wearing jeans, a black T-shirt, a Hoosiers ball cap, and wraparound sunglasses. Inside, tools, vehicle cleaning products, and various accessories were arranged on rows of shelves, but all of the customers were at the counter at the back of the store. Philip strolled back to the counter and sat on a stool to wait his turn. Behind the counter were shelves crammed with boxes of car parts.

The counterman finished ringing up a skinny, sunburned man with a large dip of snuff in his front lip and turned to Philip. "How can I help?"

"I need a pair of mini-spike strips."

"Not much call for those. Let me see if we have any." He turned to the inventory computer. "Okay." He looked at Philip. "You're in luck. I've got two kinds. I've got a three-foot strip with multiple spikes, and I've got this pocket-size job with two spikes."

"Can I see the two-spike?"

The man nodded, glanced at the computer for the shelf number, and then walked back into the rows of shelves. He came back with a small box, opened it, and set the mini-spike strip on the counter. Two two-inch spikes stuck up from the base. "You have to set it right up against the tire, so it's not good for keeping trespassers off your property. And if you're not law enforcement, and you use one of these babies in a public area, you'll be liable for damages."

"I understand. These are exactly what I need. Give me two of them."

"Cash or charge?"

"Cash."

Philip carried the boxes out to the Highlander. "Did they have what we need?" Carrie asked.

"Yes. If the slavers are waiting for us at the VA, these will be worth every penny."

"YES, SISSY," Isabel said, "as soon as I hear from him, I'll tell him." She hung up the phone. She felt a strangely inappropriate sense of relief. Crime scene investigators were at the dental office, and the receptionist didn't know where John was.

Isabel wrung out the dishrag and began wiping the kitchen island counter. When the phone had rung in the middle of the night and John had told her it was the security company calling about the burglar alarm at the office for the second time in just a week, she hadn't believed him. She'd thought for sure it must be a signal from a girlfriend. The burglar alarm never went off, and he was still acting suspiciously, even if he was back to helping the soccer coach.

Then this morning, when he wasn't in bed beside her, she'd thought the worst. She'd called his phone, and there was no answer. But now it was clear that there had been a break-in at the office. And he was missing work, something he would never do. So there probably wasn't a girlfriend. But there had to be something else, something much worse.

She started loading the dishwasher. Not a girlfriend. Not a lawsuit —that wouldn't keep him from work. Gambling? John wouldn't even buy a lottery ticket. Was he sleeping with men? She'd read something about that—or was it on an afternoon talk show? Guy figures out he's gay, starts acting erratically because his emotions are all over the place. But what would that have to do with the break-in? She put the detergent in the dishwasher and closed the door. The landline phone at the end of the kitchen counter rang.

"Hello."

"Isabel. I'm so glad I caught you."

"Where are you, John? Sissy called."

"This is so crazy, Isabel. You're not going to believe this. I've been arrested."

"Arrested?"

"When the cops searched the office last night, they found the safe open and a bunch of illegal pills."

"Pills in your safe?"

"I know. It's completely crazy. They think the pills are mine."

She sat down on a stool at the island. "You've been arrested for drugs?"

"It's all a big mistake. Really."

"Is that why you've been acting so strange? Are you an addict? What have you gotten yourself into?"

"I'm innocent, Isabel. I tried to call Kosinski, but he isn't in yet. Can you call him, tell him what's happened, ask him to come down here and get me out?"

"Okay. I'll call him. But I don't believe a word you're saying. Before this is over, you're going to tell me the truth."

LATER THAT AFTERNOON, Robin sat at her kitchen table, her arm in a sling and her laptop open in front of her, working on the Pollock story. Her smartphone was on speaker. "That's right, Tim. A source told me that Pollock has been arrested. I verified it with the police department. Charges are pending."

"So this is tomorrow's front page. Can you handle this on your own? Do you need someone to help with the writing? I could send Stacy over."

"I'm fine. I'll have it to you before five o'clock."

"Are you sure?"

"I'm almost done. More typos than usual."

"Okay, then. Pollock and his pill mill are part one."

"When we connect Pollock to Anderson, this story is going to explode."

"One day at a time," Tim replied. "I'll be looking for your email. And then you're going to take a few days off."

"I need to stay on Pollock."

"He's in jail. And you've already done the research on the fake OxyContin. So we're in a holding pattern until he makes his deal or Peanut Frazier comes out of his coma. Get some rest." He ended the call.

Robin sat back and closed her eyes. Her shoulder was pounding with her pulse. Maybe she should have stayed in the hospital one more day. But nothing was going to stop this story. Anderson was her next target. The pills from Pollock's office were the same counterfeit pills as the ones left in her kitchen. That was provable. But you could find those pills all over town. Peanut Frazier, the man who'd tried to kill her, supposedly worked for Dylan Anderson. Maybe Frazier would admit to trying to fake her suicide, and to planting the pills in her kitchen. But even that wouldn't be enough proof if he or Pollock weren't willing to implicate Anderson. There had to be more physical evidence. She turned back to her laptop.

After she emailed the story to Tim, while she was lying on the sofa waiting on Joel to bring Mexican take-out, her smartphone rang. It was a number she didn't know. "Hello?"

"Hi, Robin," Carrie said. "I've got you on speaker."

Robin sat up. "I'm surprised to hear from you."

"How's the shoulder?"

"Hurts."

"Did you write up that breaking and entering at Pollock's office?"

"How do you know about that?"

"How do you think?"

"Why did you do it?"

"Needed to speed things up. Got tired of waiting."

"So how does getting Pollock arrested help you?"

Philip came on the line. "Robin, we didn't call to give away our trade secrets."

"Why are we talking now?"

"Can you hold up the Pollock story for one day?"

"Why would I do that?"

"We just need a day."

"I think, right now, that you're the ones who owe me a favor, not the other way around."

"Just thought we'd ask."

"It's not possible. We've got to break the story before the TV or radio. It'll be in tomorrow's paper, above the fold."

"Had to try," Philip said. "Keep your eyes open. There're going to be a lot of new developments in your story over the next few days."

THE NEXT MORNING, the *Cornwell Herald* featured Robin's investigation of illegal OxyContin use in the area, culminating in the details of the pill mill being operated by Pollock. The newspaper lay on Anderson's desk as he sat in his office at A-Okay Autobody, talking with Smith.

"What do you want done about Peanut and Pollock?" Smith asked.

"Peanut's not talking," Anderson said. "He might not even make it out of intensive care. And we can't do anything about Pollock until he gets out on bail."

"Might be too late then."

"He's got a family. He doesn't want to put them in jeopardy."

"Okay."

"That whole story just doesn't add up. Somebody broke in, took the money and left the drugs. That's a set-up. Why would anyone target Pollock? This has to go back to that murder-for-hire scam."

"We dealt with that."

"We got one guy. Who are those two who've been helping Simons? Why are they here? This situation would be funny if it was happening to someone else."

"We don't know if they're the ones."

"At this point, I don't care. We can't kill Simons anymore. She's just too hot. And the info's out in public now anyway. But that man and woman? Why haven't Dougie and Tom found them? Why do I still have questions? Why aren't they out in the state park digging their own graves?"

ISABEL SAT IN THE KITCHEN, her tears falling on the front page of the *Cornwell Herald* as she read the story again. *Local dentist: drug dealer*. Their entire life—the house, the cars, the island vacations—was built on a lie. It would have been so much better if he'd actually been cheating on her. She thought about how afraid she'd been of losing him. She'd been such a fool. She wouldn't be able to face any of their friends. How could she tell Kitty and Johnny what their father had done? Would they find out at school? Maybe she should go get them. The land line phone rang.

"Hello."

"Isabel."

"You bastard."

"That newspaper story is a lie."

"How stupid do you think I am? What you've done to me and the kids—" She started bawling.

"I can't explain right now, but if you give me a chance, when I get out of here, I'll tell you everything. You'll see I'm innocent."

She slammed the phone down, pulled several tissues from the box on the counter, held them to her face with both hands and sobbed.

MIDAFTERNOON, Philip and Carrie circled Veterans Memorial Park in a stolen Chevy Silverado. The van was at its usual place, the customers were coming and going, and a few families with young children were snacking near the fountain. On the far side of the park, to one side of a huge oak, Carrie spotted two of the traffickers in a black Ford F-150.

"There're our guys."

Philip nodded. He drove down a side street, turned around and parked in front of an ice cream and coffee shop with a view of the rear of the F-150. "The Dodge Ram ought to be along in about forty minutes."

"The traffickers are not just going to tail us. We've already killed two of them."

"Yes, but they're not going to be running and gunning in the park. They'll want to catch us on the move."

"Must think we're stupid."

"Doesn't matter. They won't be following us."

Philip reached into the duffel bag sitting on the console between them and pulled out the mini-spike strips.

"Think those'll really work?"

"If they're placed right."

"I've only ever seen the long ones the cops lay across the street to stop a getaway car."

"Because these little ones have to be so carefully placed. You ready?"

She brought her AR-15 rifle up into her lap. "Go ahead."

He got out of the Silverado and walked along behind the cars parked in the metered parking spots surrounding the park, ducking down before he would be seen in the traffickers' rear-view mirror. He squatted behind their right wheel and pushed the mini-spike strip up under the tire, making sure it was tightly positioned. Then he crept over to the left wheel. The F-150's passenger door opened. Philip crawled under the truck. The door shut. He saw men's shoes. The man, a bruiser with a shaved head, walked across the street and into a pizza place. Philip slid out from under the truck, set the other mini-spike strip against the left rear tire, and moved at a crouch until he was three cars away. Then he stood up, walked to the corner, crossed the street with the walk light, and ended up at the Silverado just as the bruiser was coming out of the pizza place with a takeout box and a soft drink.

The trafficker looked both ways, crossed the street, and got back in the F-150 without noticing the mini-spike strips. Carrie laid her rifle back down on the floorboard. "Thought for a moment I was going to have to go loud."

"Me too," Philip said.

They drove around the park to their usual observation point, put on their Kevlar, and waited. The Dodge Ram arrived right on schedule, made a pickup, and drove away. They followed. As they made their first turn, they heard the sound of a tire blowing out.

"Sounds like the mini-spike strip worked," Carrie said.

"Hope it's a good omen."

Meanwhile, Pollock was standing at one of the phones in the hallway of the jail in the basement of the police station, talking with Anderson. "I'm still in jail. My lawyer hasn't gotten me out yet."

"Don't worry, we'll take care of you."

"I don't see how. I'm going to lose my license. I'm ruined."

"Maybe. Or you could get off, and the dental board could put you on probation."

"How could that happen?"

"Take a deep breath. Think of your family. Don't tell the cops anything."

"Everybody who's seen the newspaper story thinks I'm guilty. When I spoke to my wife, she couldn't stop crying."

"We're putting our lawyer on this. He's a magician when it comes to this sort of thing. He'll be in touch with your lawyer to find a way to get you out. Has anyone bothered you in jail?"

Pollock looked down the hallway to the day room. "No."

"That's the way it's going to stay. We look out for our people."

The Dodge Ram made the usual downtown street pickup, and continued across town to the strip mall where the Buick was waiting. "Just like clockwork," Philip said.

"Pull up in front of the Subway."

They watched the redhead get out of the Buick and lean back against the front bumper, a manila envelope in her hand. The Dodge Ram pulled up beside her and the dark-haired man got out, all smiles. Philip and Carrie put on their ski masks. Philip floored the Silverado. It rolled up fast and screeched to a stop. They jumped out with their AR-15 rifles trained on the man and woman. The man was reaching behind his waist.

"Don't do it," Carrie yelled.

Philip pointed with his rifle. "On the ground now!"

The redhead was shaking. She got down on her hands and knees, the envelope still in her hand.

The man brought his hands out in front of him and started slowly kneeling. "You're making a mistake."

"They always say that," Philip replied. He pushed the man onto his belly, took the revolver from the back of the man's waistband, put it into his jacket pocket, and stood on the man's back with one foot. "Move and die." He glanced at Carrie. "Make the collection, baby."

Carrie took the envelope from the woman and took the other two envelopes from off the seat of the Ram. She tossed them into the Silverado. Then she turned to the redhead. "Get up."

The woman stood up, holding herself, tears ruining her makeup.

"Car keys," Carrie said.

"My purse is in the car."

"No gun?"

She shook her head. "No gun."

"You do what you're told, you'll come out of this without a scratch. No one can blame you for this screwup. Get the car keys."

Carrie kept her rifle trained on the redhead while she got the car keys. Then she grabbed her arm, led her to the trunk, and opened it. Inside was an old blanket and a jumble of loose items. "Get in and stay quiet until you hear us drive away."

She started to step back. "I don't want—"

"Get in." Carrie pointed with her rifle.

The redhead climbed into the trunk. Carrie shut the lid.

Philip stepped off the dark-haired man and kicked him in the side. The man held his hands up in front of his face. "There's no reason for this."

"Really? You assholes killed our partner."

"I don't know what you're talking about."

"And you're going to want us dead before we're done."

The man tried to scramble to his feet. Philip shot him in the chest and the belly. Carrie was already sitting in the driver's seat of the Silverado. Philip climbed in the passenger's side, and she took off. After they bounced down onto the street and turned right, they pulled off their ski masks. At the next intersection, Carrie took another right, drove into a neighborhood of duplexes and one-story rentals, drove to the next major street, and turned left. They could hear the sirens in the distance.

"So far, so good. That should really piss them off."

"They'll be gunning for us."

"They'll be gunning for somebody. Who knows how long it will take them to figure out it was us? Besides, they're kind of busy right now, what with their killer in the ICU and Pollock in jail."

"The traffickers are still dogging us. We can't go back to the park."

"I know. Where do you think they originally picked up on us?"

"No idea."

"Then we'll need to stay away from the body shop and the money route as well."

"Where do you want to dump this truck?"

"It's clean, so we can just leave it when we switch to the Highlander."

BACK AT THE STRIP MALL, two police officers got out of their cruiser. They saw the man on the pavement lying in a pool of blood and heard the banging coming from the trunk of the Buick. One officer went to the dark-haired man, knelt beside him, and checked his pulse. He was dead. His partner used the driver's side trunk latch to open the trunk of the Buick. As he walked back to the trunk, a redhead climbed out, her hair disheveled and her makeup smeared.

"Ma'am," the officer said, "come over here and sit down."

He led her to the front seat of the Buick. She sat down with her legs out of the car.

"Thank God you're here," she said. "I thought for sure I was going to be murdered."

"What happened here, ma'am?"

She glanced toward the shops. The other officer was walking toward three people who were huddled near the door to Pro Cosmetics. "I was waiting here for my boyfriend. When he got out of his truck, these crazy people roared up like it was a TV show—you know, body armor, masks, military rifles."

"You'd never seen them before?"

"Never. I mean—how would I know? I couldn't see their faces."

"Didn't sound familiar?"

She shook her head.

"Okay, ma'am. You're going to need to wait here for the detective."

"Is it okay if I use my phone?"

He nodded and then went back to his cruiser.

She called A-Okay Autobody. The receptionist answered the phone. "I need to cancel my appointment."

"Would you like to rebook?"

"That won't be possible right now. I'll rebook later."

THE RECEPTIONIST STEPPED through to Anderson's office, where he and Little Jim Lee were having a meeting.

"Bonnie called. Travis won't be coming in. She can't talk now."

"Thanks." He waited for her to leave. "So Travis is dead."

"Maybe," Lee replied. "Maybe he's just shot. What we know for a fact is that he was ambushed."

"Bonnie called it in, so she must have been there."

"She won't talk."

"No, but we won't be able to find out what she knows until the police get done with her. In the meantime, we need more muscle on all our spots. We don't want to get hit anywhere else."

"I'll take care of it."

Russell Kosinski, stoop-shouldered and gray, parked his Toyota Avalon on the street in front of Pollock's house. "So here we are."

Pollock released his seatbelt. "Thanks, Russell."

"I called Isabel, so she's expecting you."

Pollock nodded.

Kosinski looked at Pollock carefully. "I don't need to tell you what to do here, do I?"

"No, I know I need to get the home team behind me."

"At least enough so that you look like a guy who made a mistake, not a career criminal whose family hates him. Family support is important."

"I'll find a way."

"Can you count on your employees? Do you know what they're going to say?"

"I don't know. I don't think they'll say anything."

"You know you're going to have to tell the police where the pills came from."

"I don't think I can do that."

"A friend tells me they're the same pills involved in overdoses all over the county. You won't have a chance of staying out of prison if you don't cooperate."

Pollock hung his head. "I've really got myself in a mess."

"But you can still help yourself. I'll call you tomorrow."

Pollock walked up the steps to his house. The nearby yards were empty, but he felt as if all his neighbors were watching him from behind their curtains. When he reached for the door handle, the door swung open. Isabel stood in the threshold and glared.

"I'm home."

She stepped to the side to let him in and shut the door behind him.

"Where are the kids?"

"At my parents." She stood with her arms folded across her chest.

"Say what you've got to say. I deserve it."

"How could you ever thought for a moment that selling drugs would be okay? Our neighbors think we're monsters. Thank God I got to the kids before their friends started texting them."

"I know it doesn't make sense now, but I was just trying to help people who needed help. They needed pain medication. And I needed to pay our bills, keep our lives afloat. I never meant for it to get out of hand. I always thought I'd stop after I built up my practice."

"But you got sued twice."

"Those were frivolous. If Russell had been my lawyer back then, I wouldn't have lost those cases."

"It's always someone else's fault." She looked away. "I don't want to be anywhere you're at. I'm going to the bedroom. You're sleeping somewhere else."

"I need fresh clothes."

"Go get them now."

LATER THAT EVENING, Bonnie sat in Anderson's office with Anderson and Lee. She recounted what happened and what she told the police.

Anderson nodded. "So you told the cops that Travis was your boyfriend?"

"There were witnesses. I didn't know what they saw, so I had to have a reason we were meeting that didn't involve money. That's all I could think of on the fly."

"Travis's wife isn't going to like it," Lee said.

"We'll smooth it over," Anderson replied. He turned back to Bonnie. "So the guy said, you assholes killed our partner?"

"Yes."

"You heard that through the trunk?"

"That's exactly what he said."

"And you're sure it was a man and a woman?"

"Yes."

"Thanks, Bonnie. You can go. Close up the shop until you hear from us."

She closed the office door as she left.

"So now we know," Lee said.

Anderson nodded. "These two were part of the murder-for-hire scam."

"Pollock really fucked us over with that one."

"We're not going to get any peace until these scammers are dead."

"The cops are everywhere."

"I don't care. Find Dougie and Tom. Tell them they don't sleep until we have the scammers."

9

LOOSE ENDS

The next morning, Philip and Carrie were sitting in a landscaping truck on the street down the block from Anderson's lake house, Kevlar on underneath their work clothes, when a blue Dodge Charger turned in the driveway.

"Robin's boyfriend and his partner," Carrie said.

"They must have connected the Dodge Ram driver to Anderson."

A few minutes later, they brought Anderson out and put him in the back of their car.

"Ouch," Carrie said. "He doesn't look like he even had a chance to drink his coffee."

"So much for killing Anderson this morning. Guess we'll have to put him on our to-do list. Here they come."

They slouched down in their seats while the cops drove by. Then Philip started the truck and drove off in the opposite direction.

"Anderson getting arrested might be good for us in the long run. We've messed up his business. The cops are on him. This could improve our chances of stealing his main stash."

"Before or after we kill him?"

"We'll just have to see how it plays."

"Think the traffickers are still going to try to get in our way?"

"If they can find us."

"What do you want to do about them?"

"They tried to kill us, and they're poking around in our business."

"We've killed two of them. How many are left?"

"Well, they sent two the second time, so maybe five or six total."

"So they left three or four with the girls?"

"That's what I'm guessing. Plus the boss."

"Six people out in the open is too many. Even worse if there's more."

"Then we'll have to even up the odds a bit."

"What have you got in mind?"

He smiled. "Maybe we can use the drug crew to kill the traffickers."

"Last time you did something like that, you had Cohen to help even up the odds."

"We don't have to kill them all. If we're well out of the way when the shooting starts, we should be fine."

ANDERSON SAT across from Marcos and Bledsoe in an interview room at the police station. A file folder sat on the table between the detectives. A video camera looked down on him from the wall above the door.

"Do you understand your rights?" Bledsoe asked.

"Yes," Anderson replied.

"What can you tell us about Travis Smith?"

"Not much. He's an employee of mine."

"Doing what?"

"Sales."

"How does that work?"

"Autobody is like any other kind of business. You can't just wait around for customers to show up, you have to go out and find them. Why am I here?"

"You haven't heard?" Bledsoe asked.

"Heard what?"

Marcos opened the file folder and pushed a photo across the table. It showed Smith, blood puddled around his body, lying on the pavement. "Mr. Smith was gunned down at a strip mall yesterday afternoon."

"Why are you showing me this?"

"His wife had to ID him."

Anderson pushed the photo back across the table.

"Do you know who did this?" Bledsoe asked.

"No."

"Let's cut the crap," Marcos said. "It looks like there's a new crew in town. They killed your guy yesterday. And they also killed two other guys three days ago."

"I don't know anything about that."

"These killings have got to stop."

"I've got nothing to do with any killing."

"You're not turning our streets into a war zone," Marcos continued.

Anderson scraped his chair back and stood up. "Are we done here? Am I under arrest?"

"No."

"Then I'll be on my way."

When Anderson walked down the front steps of the police station, his Cadillac was waiting at the curb. Lee got out of the driver's seat and came around to open the passenger's door. "Hey, boss. Your wife called. And since you didn't call Benny, I assumed you'd need a ride."

"Didn't need a lawyer. I knew they had nothing."

Lee got back behind the wheel. "You want the good news first?"

Anderson nodded.

"Peanut died. Never regained consciousness."

"He was a good kid. Just not too smart." Anderson watched a group of men in suits go into the building. "And the bad news?"

"Pollock is out on bail. His lawyer's been busy, so he's not in our pocket anymore."

"First things first. Cops just warned me about running and

gunning, but we're not going to stop until we've dealt with the scammers. Why don't we know where they're staying yet?"

"Tom and Dougie are turning over the city, boss."

"I'm tired of waiting for them. This is everybody's job until the scammers are found. So if anyone is sitting around, they need to get to work."

"I'll make the calls."

"Once we've dealt with the scammers, everything will go back to the normal peace and quiet. Then the cops won't be so touchy, and we won't have any trouble getting Pollock under control. He's got a wife, two kids, and a job he wants to keep. We apply a little pressure and he'll do what he's told."

ROBIN SAT down in a booth at the back of Junior's Roadhouse, a dimly lit tavern on the crossroads to Emeryville, about five miles south of Cornwell. "Dr. Pollock," Robin said, "I'm so glad you decided to meet with me."

"My lawyer told me not to do it."

"Like I told you on the phone, this is completely off the record. No one is going to know we talked unless you tell them."

He shrugged.

"You look a little worse for wear."

"Have you ever been in jail? It's frightening and humiliating. My wife and my kids—if we weren't broke, I think my wife would leave me." He sighed. "But I could say the same about you. How's the shoulder?"

"Healing. The bullet somehow missed the bone."

"How do you know about this place? I've driven this way a hundred times and never noticed it."

"Finding places like this is just something you learn in my profession." She took a small recorder out of her jacket pocket. "Mind if I use this? Kind of hard to take notes."

"I have your word?"

"Absolutely."

"No matter what I say?"

"No matter."

He nodded.

She turned on the recorder. "Let's start by clearing up a few things. You've been charged with operating a pill mill. Did the OxyContin come from Anderson?"

"Hypothetically—everything I'm going to say is hypothetical—a person like me could have been drawn into a relationship with a drug dealer like Anderson, if he is a drug dealer, through a desire to help his patients."

"And what about Peanut Frazier?"

"I've never met him."

"But you knew about him?"

"If a reporter was investigating the hypothetical person we're talking about, a drug boss might send someone to stop that investigation."

"Dr. Pollock, please. I was tipped off that you hired someone to kill me."

Pollock opened and closed his mouth. He looked at the front door to the tavern. "But I didn't have anything to do with Frazier. Nothing. Period. I didn't hire him, and I didn't send him after you."

"Then why did I receive the tip?"

He looked her in the eye. "Hypothetically, a person under a lot of pressure, afraid for their family, might contact a murder-for-hire website, thinking that was the only way to stay out of jail, only to find out that the website was a scam."

"A scam?"

"Yes. A place that just takes people's money and doesn't do what they're hired to do. Believe me, after I had a chance to think it through, I was glad they weren't going to do anything."

"But the drug boss found out?"

"Said he'd clean up the whole thing."

Robin studied Pollock's face. "But now you've been arrested. Are you going to take a deal?"

"My lawyer's looking at all my options. I hope to keep my dental license and stay out of prison."

"You really think that's possible?"

"That's all I have to say right now."

She turned off the recorder and slipped it into her pocket. "Thanks for meeting me. Maybe we can do another interview when you're ready to go on the record."

"Maybe."

Robin squinted in the bright light of the gravel parking lot. Anderson was the drug dealer. Frazier was his guy. And Pollock was trying his best to make himself look innocent. He was deluding himself if he really believed he could stay out of prison. And even if by some miracle he did manage to avoid jail time, the civil suits over malpractice and wrongful death would bankrupt him. She got into her car.

But if he wasn't lying about the murder-for-hire scam, that's where Philip and Carrie must have come from. Anderson going after them—killing their partner—was what brought them to town. They said as much, and now Pollock had verified their story. So that much must be true. She pulled out onto the highway and headed back toward Cornwell. It all added up. How much of this should she share with Joel?

MEANWHILE, back in Cornwell, Lee burst into Anderson's office without bothering to knock. He had a big grin on his face.

"Shut the door," Anderson said.

"We found the scammers."

"Where?"

"Budget Inn at the south interchange."

"You're sure?"

"One of our guys controls the laundry there. He got a solid description from the manager."

"Put four guys on this. They stay there until they've got them."

"Leave them where they lay?"

"No, take them alive. We've assumed they're the scammers. Maybe they're somebody else."

"Bonny said—"

"Bonny was scared. She heard someone speak through a trunk lid. I want to know for a fact who these assholes are before they die."

PHILIP AND CARRIE parked their Highlander near the main entrance to the Makepeace Valley Shopping mall, put on disguises—a gray beard, sunglasses, and the Hoosiers ball cap for Philip, and a gray wig and a large floppy hat for Carrie—and used their car computer override tablet to take a Subaru Forester parked in the employee parking near the access road. Then they made the rounds of Anderson's spots. At Veterans Memorial Park extra men were hanging around in the park near the van, looking over all the potential customers as they moved up to the van's window. Downtown, two police cruisers were in the street, lights flashing, and Anderson's guys were lying on the sidewalk in handcuffs. Out at the strip mall, the police tape was gone, the blood had been hosed off the pavement, and a Closed sign hung inside the glass door of the Pro Cosmetics Outlet. At A-Okay Autobody, the two men sitting in lawn chairs in front of the office were not reading the newspaper or looking at their phones. "We're having the desired effect," Philip said.

"I wonder how many of us he thinks we are?" Carrie replied.

"He's definitely gone into a defensive posture. Got to be costing him money."

Philip continued down Michelle Trail headed back toward Sweetwater Boulevard.

"We going to put this car back?"

"The Highlander will be safe where it is until well after the mall closes. We'll go back after it after we change motels."

"That's a little paranoid, don't you think?"

"There's no such thing as too paranoid. The slavers and Anderson are probably both looking for us by now."

A half hour later, Philip parked in front of their motel room at the

Budget Inn. The motel parking lot was already three-quarters full with the day's arrivals. "Have you got much packing to do?" he asked.

"Just my shower kit," Carrie replied. "I left everything else in my bag."

He unlocked the door. The room was freshly cleaned, and the bed made. The tip they'd left on the table was gone, and there were extra towels in the bathroom. "Shame we have to leave," Carrie said.

Philip lifted his roller case onto the bed and put his dirty clothes into the space next to his shaving kit. "Maybe the next one will be just as clean."

They gave the room the final once-over and rolled their bags out to the Subaru. After they put their bags in the back and came around the sides of the SUV to get in, two men rushed toward each of them, coming from in front and behind. Carrie jerked her door open to block the man in front of her and turned to kick the man coming from behind. He grabbed her ankle and flipped her onto the pavement. She saw stars, sucked in a breath, and started crawling under the Nissan SUV to her right, kicking as the man tried to grab her ankle again.

Meanwhile, on the other side of the Subaru, the man behind Philip grabbed him by his shoulders and banged him off the side of the Subaru while the bearded man in front of him got around the half-open door and swung at his face. Philip blocked the blow with his forearm, took a glancing blow to the chin, and stumbled back against the man behind him, all the time trying to bend down far enough to grab the Smith & Wesson .38 holstered on his ankle. The man behind him pulled him up by his shirt collar. The bearded man punched him in the gut. Philip fell forward toward the pavement and finally reached the .38. When the man behind him pulled him up again, he shot the bearded man in the belly, jerked around to face the man behind him, and shot him in the chest as he was pulling a Glock from his jacket.

Philip turned toward the other side of the Subaru. He couldn't see Carrie. The two men over there were pulling guns. He had four shots left in his .38. Not enough firepower. He snatched up the Glock and started shooting. The men ducked behind the body of the Subaru. Philip backed away from the SUV, firing as he went. When he was two cars away, he turned and ran.

WHEN PHILIP STARTED SHOOTING, Carrie crawled out the other side of the Nissan. Shards of window glass were raining onto the pavement. She stayed low, stopped behind the rear wheel to catch her breath, and then, at the first gap in the shooting, ran across the parking lot pulling on car door handles until the passenger door popped open on an old Previa van. She slid across the seats, tore the cover off the electrical harness below the steering wheel, and hotwired the engine. When she sat up behind the wheel, Philip was gone. The two men who'd been after her were running across the parking lot toward her. She jammed the van into Drive and pushed hard on the gas pedal. One of the men tried to grab her door. She veered toward a parked car to knock him loose. She heard shots from behind her. She was gaining speed as she reached the exit to the parking lot, squealed through a right turn, and then headed for the entrance ramp to the beltway.

Once she was on the beltway and her heart rate started to come down, she noticed blood on her right hand. She glanced down at her thigh. Blood was oozing through her pants. Now that she'd noticed the wound, it started to hurt. Where was Philip? He'd been shooting at her guys—she was sure of that—she'd heard that little .38 to begin with. But where did he go while she was running for the van?

PHILIP WAS KNEELING under the camper top in the bed of a pickup truck as he watched Carrie fly by in the Previa and screech out of the Budget Inn parking lot. There were only a few more minutes before the cops would get there, but the two guys who were still on their feet weren't carrying off their wounded. They were looking between the parked cars as if they still hoped to find him. But when the sirens started to wail in the distance, one guy yelled something at the other, and then got in a four-door Toyota Tundra, which he pulled up behind the Subaru. They dragged the other two men into the back seat of the truck and drove off.

After Philip saw the Tundra take a left out of the parking lot, he dropped out of the back of the truck and scampered along the line of parked cars at a crouch, the Glock down at his side. There was no time to waste. He had seconds—not minutes—before the witnesses started coming out of their rooms to gawk at the shot-up cars. The Subaru was riddled with bullet holes, the glass all shattered, bullet casings lying everywhere, but somehow the Nissan only had its windows shattered.

He looked in the Subaru. Carrie's shoulder bag was lying on the front seat. He couldn't take their roller bags, but he wasn't leaving her ID, the car computer override tablet, or her Glock behind. He opened the car door and pulled the bag off the seat. He slipped back the way he'd come, still crouching down, until he came to the corner of the building. Then he shoved the Glock he'd taken into his jacket pocket, stood up, looped the strap of the shoulder bag in his fist like he was the husband who'd been told to hold her bag, and walked toward the Taco Bell on the corner. Pure, dumb luck. That's the only reason he and Carrie weren't trussed up and on their way to a slow, painful death. Anderson had managed to get one step ahead of them. Couldn't let that happen again. Good thing all their gear was in the Highlander. He speed-dialed Carrie.

"Where are you, baby?" she asked.

"It's good to hear your voice," he replied.

"Yours too."

"I'm on foot, in the clear."

"Want me to circle back?"

"No. I'll catch up. That was a rough couple of minutes there. Are you okay?"

"Flesh wound on my thigh. Not quite leaking. Need a bandage."

"That's all?"

"Yeah. You?"

"Pride's hurt. Got a headache. Ears still ringing a little." He walked past the Taco Bell as the first police cruiser, sirens blaring, rushed into the Budget Inn parking lot. "There go the cops. The Subaru's a dead end. I got your bag, but we lost our luggage."

"DNA and fingerprints."

"Still trying to look on the bright side. I'll pick up a first aid kit and meet you at the Highlander."

"See you soon."

ROBIN SET her home's perimeter alarm, poured herself a glass of white wine, sat down on the sofa and put her feet up. Six thirty. She was surprised she hadn't heard from Joel. She got out her phone.

"Hey, Joel."

"Hey yourself. I was just about to call you. How was your day?"

"Interesting. Can you talk?"

"Yes. I just dropped off Steve."

"I just did an off-the-record interview with you-know-who."

"Pollock?"

"I can't say. If the source is to be believed, Frazier works for Anderson."

"We sort of knew that already."

"But when this source goes public, it will be irrefutable." She took a sip of wine. "This next part is kind of wild."

"Spill."

"I've got more on why Carrie and Philip are here. The source says that they were running a dark web murder-for-hire scam and that Anderson came after them."

"A scam?"

"Taking money from suckers."

"So it's all just about payback?"

"If the source is telling the truth, the source hired Phillip and Carrie and Anderson set out to clean up his mess. At least, that's what he says."

"Sounds a little farfetched."

"Explains why they wanted info about Pollock and Anderson. Buttered me up with the sex trafficking story so I'd help them out."

"Maybe. Could be your source is blowing smoke."

"We'll see. You coming over?"

"Thought I'd pick up some Vietnamese on the way."

"I can't wait."

"Hold on. I've got a call I have to take."

A minute later, Joel came back on the line. "I'm sorry, Robin. I'm going to be awhile. There's been a shoot-out at the Budget Inn off Clancy Road. Want to see if it fits the profile of the last two gunfights."

"The T-bone at the intersection and killing in the Pro Cosmetics parking lot?"

"Yes. Not quite sure how long I'll be. You should eat without me."

"I'll wait."

"You sure?"

"You promised Vietnamese."

He hung up. She called in to the *Herald* offices. "Mikey? It's Robin. There been some shooting at the Budget Inn on Clancy Road."

"We know. Pulled it off the scanner. Stacy's on it."

"Great. I'll let you go then."

Robin sipped her wine. She wondered what the witnesses were going to say and what evidence was left at the scene. Would someone identify Philip and Carrie? She called Carrie's phone number, but it rolled over to a mailbox that hadn't been set up.

PHILIP CROSSED the street from the Taco Bell to a Days Inn, strolling along the parked cars with his phone up to his ear to obscure his face from any security cameras. A mom and dad with two preteens got out of a car on the far side of the lot and rolled their bags toward the building. He spotted an old Camry, used his lockpicks to pick the lock, and slid in behind the wheel. These pre-computer cars were so easy to take. A few minutes later, he was driving away. He stopped at a Walmart, parked away from the building, and thought for a moment.

What did they need besides the first aid kit? Carrie sounded all right. It would be worth taking a few extra minutes.

He pushed a cart down the aisle. In the pharmacy section, he picked up a camper's first aid kit, toothbrushes and shaving gear. In the household goods, he put two large bottles of bleach in the cart. In men's clothing, he picked out khaki pants and a golf shirt, in women's clothing, underwear, sweatpants, and a long-sleeve T-shirt. Finally, in the grocery section, he picked up packaged sandwiches, granola bars, a six-pack of water, and a pint of whiskey. He took it all to the self-checkout. It was the tail end of rush hour by the time he got back on the road and made his way across town to Makepeace Valley Shopping Mall.

Once he got to the mall, he sent Carrie a text. *Where are you?*

South side at the back of the lot by the movie theater entrance.

A movie was letting out as he spotted the Previa parked at the far end of the parking lot. He pulled into the parking place beside it, climbed into the passenger's side of the van with the first aid kit, and leaned over the console to kiss Carrie.

"I'm glad you're here," she said.

"Me too. That looks like a lot of blood."

"It always looks like a lot of blood."

"How do you want to do this?"

"Just wrap it over the pants until we get to the next motel."

"It doesn't need stitches?"

"Trust me, it's just not that big of a deal."

He bandaged her leg. "That should hold until you can get your pants off."

"You just can't wait, can you?"

He smiled. "I also brought you a change of clothes."

"That sounds scary."

"They're clean, that's all I'm promising."

"What do you want to do about this van?"

"We're going to bleach it. Then we can just leave it here. Maybe the cops won't notice it for a couple of days."

He walked Carrie to the Camry and laid his jacket on the seat for her to sit on just in case her bandage leaked. Then he went back to the van and poured bleach all over the interior where they'd sat. When he was finished, he left the bleach bottles in the van and locked the doors. Then he jogged around the front of the van and got into the Camry.

"You smell like a laundromat," Carrie said.

"Better than the alternative."

They drove around the mall to where they'd parked the Highlander. Carrie climbed into the SUV while Philip wiped down the steering wheel, console, and doors of the Camry. Then he got into the Highlander and backed out of the parking spot. "So far, so good."

Carrie looked up from her smartphone. "There's a Holiday Inn Express at an exit we haven't stayed at."

"Great." He gave her a glance. "You look completely trashed."

"I was crawling under a car."

"You'll have to sneak in."

He drove away from the mall and onto Sweetwater Boulevard. Night was coming on, the sunset dimming in the west. "We were way too lucky with that last fiasco."

"I know. Heavy gear and money in the Highlander, neither of us captured or dead. And you got my shoulder bag."

"We can't count on any more luck. And the cops have our bags and the Subaru. So we can add them to the list of people who are after us."

"But we're not running."

"No, not yet. I think we've still got time to take care of Anderson."

Marcos picked up Bledsoe on his way to the south interchange. "This better be worthwhile," Bledsoe said. "I'm supposed to be at my son's baseball game."

"These crime calls are never convenient, are they? Always early or late or over lunch or dinner."

"No problem for the single man."

"I'm supposed to be with Robin right now."

"What? She run out of things to write about?"

Marcos pulled into the Budget Inn parking lot. Two patrol officers were working the perimeter. Inside the police tape, there were shell casings and blood on the ground, but no bodies. Two CSI techs were dusting for fingerprints in a shot-up Subaru. Detective Lewis was standing in front of a pock-marked Nissan, sweat beading on his bald head.

"Hey, Troy," Marcos said.

"Hey, Joel, Steve. What're you two doing here?"

"Just wanting to know if this is part of the drug war."

"I've got three very consistent witnesses. A man and a woman were getting in the Subaru. Four big guys attacked them. Gunfire like World War Three. Two of the attackers went down. The woman escaped in a Toyota van. The man disappeared. Two of the attackers loaded the other two in a Toyota truck. No one got the license plate number. The owner of the van, an older guy going on a fishing trip, doesn't know how he's going to get home."

"Who owns the Subaru?"

"It's registered to Jane Lamott, who manages the Game Time shoe store at the mall. She swore her vehicle was in the parking lot until we made her go out and check."

"Nissan?"

"Another motel guest."

"But you're pulling fingerprints?"

"Yeah. And there's luggage in the back."

Marcos turned to Bledsoe. "So the shootout in the intersection, the murder at the strip mall, and now this, all involving an unidentified man and woman."

"Hard to believe it's a coincidence," Bledsoe replied.

Lewis slapped his notebook shut. "So what are you saying? Does this case belong to the drug task force? Are you going to take it off my hands?"

Marcos frowned. "We're just working a theory, Troy. Let's see what CSI finds out."

. . .

Philip checked in to the Holiday Inn Express, where he took a room with two queen beds on the second floor in the middle of the hall. Carrie slipped in a side door so she wouldn't be seen by the receptionist. After they got into the room, she pulled the bedspread off the nearest bed and lay on top of the sheet. "I'm so exhausted."

Philip locked the door. "Don't get too comfortable. We've still got to get you cleaned up."

He went into the bathroom and turned on the shower. Then he came back out with a towel. "You ready for this?"

"Let's do it."

He slipped the towel under her taped-up thigh. Then he opened the first aid kit and used the scissors to cut through the tape and cut open the pants leg.

"How does it look?"

"Not too deep. Still weeping a little. Trying to scab. How does it feel?"

"Throbbing a little."

"So shower first, then bandage."

She pulled her shirt off over her head. He tugged off her pants and underwear. "You going to need help?"

"I can stand. I'll be fine."

Philip waited in the bathroom while she showered. Afterward, she sat on the toilet lid, naked, a towel wrapped around her hair, while he knelt in front of her and cleaned the wound with antiseptic wipes.

"Almost done." He tossed the wipes into the trashcan, set a piece of sterile gauze in place and then wrapped the wound.

"Looks pretty good," she said. "Now let me see the clothes you bought me."

He handed her a Walmart bag. "It was the best I could do."

"I've set my expectations low enough."

She put on the sweatpants and T-shirt. "At least they're my size."

Philip gathered her dirty clothes and put them in the bag. "Why don't you rest, eat a sandwich, while I get cleaned up?"

Philip showered, changed into his Walmart clothes, and put his dirty clothes in the same bag as hers. Carrie was sitting against the headboard of the other bed, drinking a whiskey and water, a sandwich wrapper on the night table beside her.

"Sandwiches any good?"

"How hungry are you?"

He poured himself a whiskey. "It's been a long day. We've been pushed back on our heels. Anderson will be expecting us to reassess our situation, take some time to regroup."

"So we're pushing back hard tomorrow?"

"If we can manipulate him into going after the slavers, we're going to make him pay."

ANDERSON STOOD out in his backyard next to the decorative fence at the edge of the man-made lake, his phone up to his ear. A neighbor, standing at his grill, waived. Anderson waved back and tried to smile. Then he looked back toward the house. He could see Sally clearing the dinner dishes from the dining room table. "You don't have to repeat the whole damn thing again."

"You wanted me to explain," Lee said.

"You sent four hard guys—"

"You know them."

"They ambushed the man and the woman in a parking lot."

"Yep."

"And this is the result."

"You wanted them taken."

"That's bullshit."

"Okay."

"And now the cops are all over it."

"I thought you'd want to know right away."

"That's the first thing you're right about." Anderson ended the call. What a fiasco. A shootout at a motel in broad daylight. Travis would have never let that happen. Christ. The cops were not going to let this go. Their guy on the force wouldn't be any help at all. He started walking back toward the house. At least they hadn't left any bodies at the scene. They had some deniability. The cops had shell casings, probably some bad parking lot surveillance footage, blood, maybe some scared eyewitnesses. It was bad, but it could be worse. None of it would lead back to him. He shoved his phone back into his pocket. Fucking scammers. Rob his house. Kill Travis. And now this. Lee had been right. He'd wanted them alive. That was his mistake. He wouldn't make it again.

10

TURNING THE TABLES

The next morning, Phillip and Carrie skipped the complimentary breakfast at the Holiday Inn Express, carried their gear out to the Highlander, and went across the street to the Perkins. The morning rush was already over and they were seated at a booth in a sunny window. Their server, a young woman with a row of heart tattoos on her wrist, brought a pot of coffee with the menus. "What are you going to have?" Carrie asked.

"I'm starving," Philip said. "I'm going for the cheese omelet and hash browns with a side of bacon."

"How about if I order pancakes and we share?"

"Great."

Their server swung back around to take their order. They sipped their coffee. "Ready to plan the day?" Carrie asked.

"Sure."

"We still going to push Anderson and the sex traffickers together?"

"That's the plan. If they're still here and he'll bite."

"We need better clothes. I need makeup and a full shower kit. And clothes for night work."

Philip nodded. "You're right. And we need a few props."

Their server brought their food. They spent a few minutes sharing the omelet and pancakes and poured more coffee.

"So we go shopping," Philip said. "Buy new bags, the works. That way, when we leave town, we'll have everything we need for running hard and fast."

MARCOS GOT off the phone with Jerry Gordon. A man and a woman shooting it out with four mopes at close range and we had nothing to go on. The only traceable fingerprints from the Subaru belonged to the owner. The luggage found in the back contained the usual items —clothes, underwear, shower stuff. The parking lot surveillance footage wasn't good enough to show anyone's faces. Rewinding the surveillance to earlier in the day showed what appeared to be the same couple getting out of a Toyota Highlander, but it didn't show the plates. Three shootings in broad daylight in four days. The captain was spitting nails. Maybe Robin's theory wasn't so implausible. He called her.

"Hey, Robin."

"Hey, handsome."

"You got a minute?"

"What's up?"

"I just talked with Jerry Gordon. That couple you told me about—Philip and Carrie—what do they look like?"

"You've seen them."

"In the distance in the dark. How tall are they?"

"She's about my height. He's a little over six feet, I'd guess. What's this about?"

"Off the record?"

"Of course."

"There were two suitcases in the back of the Subaru. They don't belong to the owner."

"So you think they belong to the couple who fought off the goons and escaped."

"Got to be. Now Philip and Carrie took you to the Paradise Truck Plaza?"

"Yeah."

"What were they driving?"

"I think it was a Toyota Highlander."

"Are you sure? I know they were driving an SUV when they dropped you off at your house, but I'm not sure it was a Highlander."

"Pretty sure. What's this about?"

"Do you really believe that Philip and Carrie would roll into town to take on Anderson?"

"Maybe it's just a coincidence that bad guys started getting shot up after they arrived. I just don't think Pollock made up that part of his story about trying to hire a killer on the dark web. It sounds too stupid naive to be a lie. I'm sure he massaged other parts of the story to make himself look better, but I don't think he made the whole thing up."

"Will you help me find them?"

"Are you starting to believe my theory, Joel?"

"If you're right, they've shot five people that we know of. And they're gunning for Anderson's crew. It's only a matter of time before bystanders get hurt."

"I might be able to help you."

"So you're in?"

"Let me think." The line went quiet for a moment. "Joel? Here's the deal. I'll help you find them, and you'll keep me completely in the loop on everything you turn up on Anderson."

"Jesus, Robin, I'd hate to be someone you're not sleeping with."

"Joel, one thing's got nothing to do with the other. And I've been playing straight with you. You wouldn't even be looking for them if I hadn't told you about what Pollock said."

"Okay, I hear you. You've got a deal."

Later that afternoon, Philip and Carrie drove south on Sweetwater Boulevard into the downtown, turned right, and continued into a rundown neighborhood of once elegant houses, until they came to Stafford Circle. Two hard-muscled men sat on the wraparound porch. Two Suburbans sat in the driveway. "They're not working the girls at all. The police crackdown must be killing them."

Carrie studied the men. "No guns on those two on the porch. Wonder if they're planning on leaving town?"

"If they were planning on leaving, they wouldn't have been after us the day before yesterday. They would already be gone. They're made to fit for our plan."

That evening, Philip and Carrie sat on the bed in their room at the Holiday Inn Express eating drive-through hamburgers and watching the local news highlights of the recent upsurge in violent crime and the police response. "We need to finish up and get out of town," Carrie said. "The cops are already using overtime."

Philip crushed his burger wrapper and tossed it into the trashcan. "Think Anderson is ready to play?"

Carrie shrugged. "Let's find out."

Philip called Anderson and put the phone on speaker.

"Hello?"

"Hear you're looking for us."

"Who is this?"

"You know who we are. You came after us and now we've come to get even."

"We need to straighten out our problems."

"How do you want to do that?"

"We messed with you, you messed with us, it's bad for business. It's time for it to stop."

"I know why you want to stop. Cops are all over you. You need extra muscle on the street. But we're doing just fine."

"Look, it wasn't personal. Just business. We don't care about you. We just needed to shut up the reporter."

"That really worked, didn't it? Now we're all out time and money. And we're taking ours back in aggravation."

"Maybe I could give you an incentive to leave. Some money to cover your inconvenience."

"How much incentive?"

"Twenty thousand."

"You joking?"

"Twenty-five."

"Thirty."

"And you're gone?"

"Like we were never here."

"How do I know you'll really leave?"

"You'll just have to take that chance."

"That's it, then. Thirty thousand. We can meet tomorrow."

"No. We meet tonight."

"That's pretty short notice to get the money together."

"Please, you've got that much in petty cash. I'll call with the location at ten. You come in person. And we'll have our guys with us, so don't try anything." He ended the call.

"Nicely handled," Carrie said.

"Thanks."

She sniggered.

"What?"

"What if he's really planning to pay us off?"

"I hope not. That would wreck our plan." He scooted off the bed. "Come on. We need to find a car for tonight and set the Highlander for after."

By 9:00 p.m., the rain was pelleting the windows of their motel room. Philip and Carrie had checked over their AR-15 rifles and made sure the extra magazines were full. They weren't taking any chances tonight. They moved casually down the hallway to the elevator, keeping an eye out for anyone suspicious, raincoats on over their body armor and tactical clothing, Philip carrying the rifles in the duffel with the extra gear.

Carrie slid behind the wheel of the Ford Escape they'd picked up from the Cornwell Medical Center employee parking lot. She circled the block before they got on the beltway just to make sure they weren't being followed. Then she got off at the next exit and drove north on Sweetwater Boulevard into the downtown, finally arriving at Stafford Circle. The rain had slowed. The two Suburbans were still in the driveway of the traffickers' house, and one of the guys from that afternoon sat on the glider on the porch. "Looks good."

They drove a block away and parked on the street facing the circle. Philip got out his phone and called Anderson.

"Where's the meet?" he asked.

Philip gave him the Stafford Circle address.

Twenty minutes later, a four-door Tacoma truck and two Ford Expeditions sped past them and turned into Stafford Circle. Carrie drove up to the circle entrance. Anderson's men were piling out of the truck and SUVs, firing at the house as they ran across the yard, their gun muzzle flashes strobing in the dark. The traffickers were returning fire. Thunder boomed, and the rain became a downpour. Men were slipping and falling in the wet grass as they rushed the porch. Philip handed Carrie a burner phone. "You're up."

Carrie called 911. She spoke in a panic. "Help. Home invasion. They're trying to kill us all." She gave the address, and then tossed the phone out onto the grass without ending the call.

"Now we're in business," Philip said.

"You think Anderson brought all his guys?"

"We're about to find out."

She drove just above the speed limit, turned left onto Sweetwater Boulevard, and moved aggressively through traffic, pushing the yellow lights as they sped north. After she turned onto Beaverdale Road, she slowed down, watching for cars backing out of driveways in the dark.

"Next right," Philip said.

Carrie turned onto Michelle Trail. All the other businesses were closed for the night. No lights, no cars, no employees, but at A-Okay Autobody, the office light was on. She turned off her headlights and rolled off the pavement onto the grass next to a bank of huge yew bushes. The rain was falling steadily. The night was black. She opened the liftback. They tossed their raincoats inside and picked up their AR-15 rifles and the duffel of tools. The eight-foot chain-link gate was padlocked. Philip snapped the chain with a pair of bolt cutters.

They inched the gate open just enough to slip through and crept down to the building, avoiding the ring of light from the pole lamp in front of the garage entrance. They peeked in the lit window to the front office. A small Asian man wearing a T-shirt and jeans sat on a sofa watching TV, a pistol on the coffee table in front of him. Philip and Carrie sneaked around to the back side of the building. No one. They crept back around to the front. As the man was changing channels with the TV remote, Philip kicked in the door. The man dropped the remote and lunged for the pistol, snatching it up as he rolled over the table. Philip and Carrie both fired, riddling the table and the man with holes. Then they swung their rifles around, silent, checking the perimeter, listening for running footsteps or voices, but all they heard was the rain. Philip prodded the man with his foot before he picked up the man's pistol and dropped it into the duffel. Then he pushed his wet hair back off his forehead and looked down the hallway.

There were three offices. The first one had two desks, desktop computers, full in-baskets. The second one had one desk and comfy chairs. The third one had a heavy deadbolt. Philip shot through it. Inside, boxes of chemicals and paper goods were stacked on shelves, and a six-foot by three-foot floor safe sat against the opposite wall. Philip glanced back at Carrie. "Watch the front."

She disappeared into the outer office. Philip dropped the duffel and set his rifle beside it in easy reach. This was a good safe, but not that good. No thumbprint reader, no electronics to overcome, just an old-school combination dial, as if it was here to keep the employees from stealing, not to keep a safecracker out. He took a piece of paper and a pencil out of his pocket. Then he gave the dial a spin, took a few easy breaths, and fell into his pattern. He wrote down the first click. This safe was going to take a few tries, but he had plenty of time. Carrie had his back. There was nothing for him to think about except opening the safe.

A few minutes later, he swung the door open. The lower shelves were stacked with gallon-size plastic bags of pills, while banded bundles of money filled the shelves above. Philip reached into the duffel for a Tyvek bag, shook it out, and shoved the bundles of money in without counting them. He stood up, put the duffel straps over one shoulder and the Tyvek bag straps over the other, and held his rifle with both hands as he moved back down the hall. Carrie was waiting at the office door. She looked over her shoulder.

"We good to go?" he asked.

"It's all clear," she said.

He slipped the Tyvek bag off his shoulder and tossed it to her. "Let's get out of here."

The rain was bucketing down, splashing in the puddles. They moved quickly across the parking lot, straining to hear any suspicious sounds and watching for any sudden movement, but all they heard was a single car whooshing by on the wet road. No one was waiting to ambush them at the chain-link gate. The Ford was still sitting where they left it beside the yews.

They drove away, taking it easy, driving east toward Griffith Street. "How much was in the safe?" Carrie asked.

"Don't know. A lot. All mixed denominations. I left the drugs."

"So we dump this car, collect our gear, and move motels?"

"You got it. We find out how many of Anderson's guys are dead or in jail and wait for the best chance to kill him."

"This has been tricky all the way along."

"Should have passed on Pollock's murder-for-hire money. Thought he was a complete idiot," Philip replied.

"Which he is."

"But the scam was too good to be true. Didn't think Pollock would have a partner to protect him."

"Who could have known?" Carrie asked.

"If we'd made a different choice, Merlin would still be alive."

"Yeah, and if we'd sent him for take-out, we might be dead right now. Merlin knew the risks. There's nothing we can do about that now except try to make things right."

. . .

IN THE MEANTIME, Anderson's crew had made their way into the house. Women were screaming and running out the back. Three of Anderson's men were lying in the yard. One trafficker lay bleeding in the entry, another on the stairs. Anderson was moving through the rooms, three of his men around him, looking for the scammers, the man and woman who had caused him so much trouble, and killing whoever they found. But what he was seeing didn't make sense. The house was full of women, women's clothes, makeup and toiletries. This was a pimp's house.

He heard sirens on the street and looked out a window. Two police cruisers had just squealed up, blocking their SUVs. He turned to the three men who were with him. "Let's get out of here."

They ran down the stairs and through the kitchen into the backyard, where the wind whipped the rain into their faces. A woman wearing a bathrobe was squeezing through two missing boards in the back fence. Anderson pointed with his pistol. One of his guys broke out another board. They climbed through the fence into a backyard overgrown with weeds. The back of the two-story house in front of them had a hole in the roof. The steps were missing a tread and a railing, and the windows were boarded up. Anderson turned to one of his men. "Manuel. Find a car. Anything that will get us out of here."

Manual hurried off. Anderson and the other two men moved around to the side of the house to get under the roof overhang. Anderson took out his phone and called the body shop. There was no answer. He called Little Jim's cellphone number. Nothing. What a clusterfuck. Little Jim wouldn't have left the body shop without leaving someone there. And he would have answered his phone. Everything about this setup stank. Where were the scammers? Who were these pimps they'd been fighting?

He called another number. "Kenny. Go to the body shop. Call me when you get there."

They heard a short beep from a car horn and hurried around the house. Manuel was sitting behind the wheel of an ancient Volkswagen, its windshield wipers screeching back and forth. They piled in.

"It was the best I could do, boss."

"Just get us out of here."

THE RAIN HAD STOPPED by the time Philip and Carrie arrived at the parking lot of the city league soccer field where they had left their Highlander. "We still putting the Ford back?" Carrie asked.

"Why not? It's not dinged up and we've been wearing gloves."

After they transferred the money and their gear from the Ford Escape, Philip followed Carrie back to the hospital parking lot. Someone else had parked in the space they'd taken the Ford from, but she found an empty spot just a few spaces farther from the employee entrance.

"I'd like to see their expression when they're looking for their car in the wrong place," Philip said.

"They probably won't notice," Carrie replied. "What motel do you want to move to?"

"I'm thinking about that. If Anderson's still alive, we're not going to catch him alone after tonight. So we're going to need to lure him into an ambush. We don't want to make it too hard for them to find us, and the Holiday Inn Express is a pretty strong location."

"Maybe he's already dead."

"I'm not counting on it."

THE VOLKSWAGEN HAD JUST TURNED onto Sweetwater Boulevard when Kenny called Anderson back. "Little Jim is dead. The safe is open and the money's gone."

"What about the product?"

"Looks like it's all still there."

"Meet us at Cornwell Tech."

Anderson ended the call. The scammers had played him, taken his money, cost him some good men. And when the cops got finished processing that house, they'd connect some of the dead men to him. At least the vehicles were clean. He couldn't do anything about the cops, but there had to be a way he could still outmaneuver the scammers, kill them and get his money back. There had to be. They weren't leaving here, that was for sure. They wanted to humiliate him and murder him. Maybe he could use that.

Kenny, a tall black man with rows of rings on his hands, was waiting in his Avalon in the west parking lot of Cornwell Technical College when the Volkswagen pulled up and Anderson and three men climbed out.

"What do you want to do about the Volkswagen?" Manuel asked.

"Leave it. We're all wearing gloves," Anderson said.

Anderson got into the front and the others got into the back. Kenny put the car in gear and headed toward Sweetwater Boulevard.

"So Little Jim is dead?"

"Full of holes."

"And the money is gone."

"Yes."

They drove along in silence for a few minutes. "What do you want to do about Little Jim?" Kenny said.

"His wife will want a funeral," Anderson replied, "so we'll have to dump him somewhere and tip the cops. Fucking shame. He was a good man."

"Not a gunman, though."

"No, never was any good with a gun."

"But he knew computers," Manuel said.

"You got that right," Anderson said. "He knew computers."

Anderson turned to Kenny. "When we get back, I want you to call whoever didn't roll out with us. We need everyone. The guys the cops didn't snag will be drifted in. We all stay together until we've settled with these bastards."

"Even the corner guys?"

"No. Not them. Make sure they're armed up. We need to keep earning."

. . .

At the Holiday Inn Express, Philip and Carrie sat at the table in their room doing a preliminary count on the A-Okay safe money, adding up the bundles. "What does that make?" Philip asked.

"It totals up at one hundred, seventy-two thousand, more or less."

"More or less." He laughed.

"This is definitely vacation money."

"Vacation money? This is Four Seasons resort money. And on a three-way split, added to the other cash we've been taking, Merlin's family is going to end up with a nice cushion."

"So all that's left is killing Anderson."

Philip nodded. "It won't take long for his guys to find us."

"Where do you want to stash the money in the meantime?"

"Too much money for a PO box. And we don't want to set up a bank safe deposit box, because we might not be able to get it quickly enough if we need to run."

"How about if we have an alarm and engine kill switch installed in the Highlander and use it as a rolling safe deposit? It's worked before. We could park it in a parking deck with surveillance cameras and an attendant."

"It's risky—I hate to put the entire score at risk—but I think you're right, it's our best shot."

In the morning, Carrie googled a specialty auto parts installer. Philip made the call and got an afternoon appointment. Then they got dressed for the day, Carrie's Glock in her shoulder bag and Philip's .38 in his ankle holster. They put some clothes into the dresser. Then they shouldered the money and their gear and pulled their roller bags down the hallway to the elevator. No one suspicious was hanging around the reception counter or the breakfast buffet.

The parking lot was half-empty, most serious travelers having made an early start. They tossed the duffels containing their gear and the money into the back seat and put their roller bags into the floor of the back seat before they climbed in. "Everything's too quiet," Carrie said.

"I know," Philip replied, "Ought to enjoy it, but I can't."

"Waiting for the shoe to drop."

. . .

MEANWHILE, Anderson walked across the parking lot of A-Okay Autobody to meet Detectives Marcos and Bledsoe as they got out of their Dodge Charger. "Here to harass me some more?"

"Your crew was involved in a gunfight last night," Bledsoe said.

"My crew?" Anderson gestured toward the autobody techs working in an open bay. "These guys are the only crew I have."

"Could we talk inside?" Marcos glanced toward the brand-new steel office door.

"Sorry, we've got renovations going on. It's a mess."

Bledsoe took three photos out of a manila envelope and handed them to Anderson. "Know these guys?"

Anderson looked at the photos. The Stafford Circle shootout. The scammers really screwed them there. Got three guys shot up and used it as a diversion to rob the safe. Three men lying in their own blood. Three men whose families were going to have to be paid off. "I don't know. If you could give me their names, I could have one of the girls check our employment records." He handed the photos back. "Sorry I can't be of more help."

Bledsoe handed him another photo. "How about this one?"

Anderson blinked. Little Jim lying in a ditch near a bus stop. He really owed the scammers for that one. That one was personal. He shrugged. "Maybe. Like I said, give me the name and one of my girls will look in our records."

"Have you got any guys left, Mr. Anderson?"

"I've never had any trouble hiring help."

Marcos continued. "Still going to pretend you don't know what we're talking about? Maybe Dr. Pollock will be able to help us understand what's going on."

"Pollock? The guy you arrested? I don't have any idea."

"We'll be in touch."

Anderson watched the detectives get back into their Dodge and drive away. Pollock, the scammers, pressure from the cops—everything was getting too complicated. They couldn't kill the cops. They were going to kill the scammers. Kill them and get the money back. But Pollock? Was he getting out of hand? He'd managed to get caught with his product. He'd been seen talking to the reporter at Junior's Roadhouse. What did he tell her? Was he cooperating with the police as well, or just trying to spin his way out of his trouble? Wouldn't it just be simpler to kill him, too? He wouldn't be able to move product anymore. Wouldn't be good for anything. After the scammers. That would be the time.

MARCOS AND BLEDSOE drove back downtown to the police station. "He was lying," Bledsoe said. "Wasn't even trying to be convincing."

"And something's going on at the body shop. That renovation looked like it got started this morning."

"And why get in a beef with some pimps? He doesn't run girls, at least as far as we know."

"I told you what Pollock told Robin, that Philip and Carrie are behind all this."

"I still don't buy it."

"What if we could connect them to the murders Rodriguez is working?"

"The T-bone in the intersection?"

"Exactly." Marcos got out his cell phone. "Mike, you having any luck with the murders you caught? I've got a theory. Meet us at the station."

PHILIP AND CARRIE ate lunch at a family-style Italian restaurant in a strip mall across from an office building. The place was noisy with office workers in a hurry to eat and get back across the street, which meant they were safe from prying eyes. At a quarter to one, they drove into a commercial zone to the southwest part of town to find Andy's Specialty Auto Installations, located between an auto parts store and an oil change shop.

The bell rang when they walked in, and the man behind the

counter, hunter's beard, ball cap, and T-shirt with company logo, looked up. "How can I help?"

"I called about getting a deluxe alarm system installed," Philip nodded.

"On the Highlander?"

He nodded.

"Pull into the open bay around back."

They drove around back and pulled into the open garage. A black man in grease-smeared coveralls came through the door at the back. "Deluxe alarm system?"

Philip nodded.

"You planning on waiting? It's going to take around three hours."

"Is there a coffee shop around here?"

"There's a Caffeination on the corner."

"So we're talking around four?"

"Maybe a little earlier."

Philip and Carrie pulled the duffel bags out of the back seat and left.

MARCOS, Bledsoe, and Rodriguez were crowded around one side of the table in an interview room at the police station. On the other side of the table, a middle-age woman with smeared mascara and dyed black hair was studying photos of the two men killed at the wreck of the Volvo and the Ford Explorer.

"You want to know if I know these guys?"

"That's right," Marcos said.

"And if I tell you the truth, make a statement, I walk out of here?"

"Like the arrest never happened."

"Both these guys worked for Lincoln."

"He was your boss?"

She nodded.

Marcos pointed at the pictures. "What are their names?"

"Sergei and Jack."

"Last names?"

"I don't know."

"So what happened here?"

"Specifically? You'd know better than me. These two grifters—that's what Lincoln thought they were—got in our business, put the reporter on us, so Lincoln sent Sergei and Jack to deal with them."

"A man and a woman."

"Yeah, two pains in the ass."

"What about the reporter? Did he send anyone after her?"

"Lincoln thought that would bring too much heat. He figured killing the grifters was enough."

Marcos glanced at Rodriguez and Bledsoe.

"Is that it? Can I go?"

"We'll get your statement typed up," Rodriguez said, "you sign it, and then you can go."

The detectives went out into the hall. "So this couple," Bledsoe said, "the grifters, are connected back to Robin and the dead kid—the OD Robin was so hot about."

Rodriguez cut in. "Okay, so now I know who the dead guys are, but who are the shooters?" He looked from Bledsoe to Marcos. "You guys know more than you're telling."

"It's all still speculation," Marcos said. "Info from a confidential informant that we're checking step by step."

"Don't worry, Mike," Bledsoe said, "you're going to know as soon as we know."

Marcos and Bledsoe walked out into the parking lot. "The story Robin told you is sounding more convincing all the time," Bledsoe said.

"The T-bone shootout was the loose end. But now we've got this couple—Robin's sources on the sex trafficking—at all three of the murders. The first one, the traffickers were after them, the second one, at the strip mall, they were after Anderson's guy, and the third one, at the Budget Inn, Anderson was hitting back. And somehow they're connected with Anderson going after the sex traffickers."

"Is that provable?"

"Is any of it provable? The T-bone shootout is all circumstantial.

Anderson's people would have to testify about the other two," Marcos said.

"If we're going to get the captain off our backs, we need to find this couple."

"The only lead we've got is that Highlander."

"We're not going to find it without the plate numbers."

WHEN PHILIP and Carrie came back to Andy's Specialty Auto Installations at 4:00 p.m., their Highlander was parked in front of the building. Carrie waited with the duffels beside the SUV while Philip went inside. The counterman looked up from his computer. "Let me get you rung up."

Philip paid with cash and the counterman handed him his receipt. "Sixty-day warranty on parts and labor."

"Great."

"Let me take you through the features."

They went outside to the Highlander. The counterman showed them how to arm and disarm the system with the remote control. "Any questions?"

"Thanks for your help," Philip said.

Philip and Carrie tossed the duffels into the back seat. After Philip merged into the rush hour traffic, he said, "Which way?"

Carrie was looking at the map app on her phone. "There's a city park northwest of here. Take the second right."

She guided him to the Shriners Park. Several cars were in the main parking lot and joggers were on a nearby trail. He turned left and drove down a gravel access road until they were behind a softball field and stopped behind a concession stand. There was no one in sight. They laid towels over their roller bags in the back seat floor. Then Carrie stood watch while Philip pulled the tire out of the wheel well and packed the cash in there—the $172,000, the $4,000 from the courier, the $3,000 from Pollock's safe, and the $70,000 from Anderson's home safe. He fixed the wheel well cover back in place, then put the tire on top and covered it with an old blanket.

"All ready?" she asked.

"We need another car."

"Airport?"

"Why not?"

They drove out to the airport and into the long-term parking. The shuttlebus was just leaving. Philip cruised the aisles. "What would you like to drive?"

"What about that Escalade?"

He stopped in the aisle. "Hand me the tablet."

She reached back into the gear duffel and pulled out the car computer override tablet.

"I'll meet you outside the gate."

She got into the driver's seat and drove out of the long-term parking lot. A few minutes later, Philip appeared in the Escalade. She pulled out behind him. They drove downtown, traveling against the end-of-work traffic, until they found the parking garage they were looking for. Philip parked on the street, got into the SUV with Carrie, and she drove into the lot, taking a ticket from the machine at the entrance. She drove up through the levels until the vehicles thinned out.

"There's our spot." Philip pointed to a parking place that was clearly covered by a surveillance camera.

Carrie pulled into the spot. They took care to keep their backs to the camera as they got out of the Highlander. Philip took their gear bag from the back seat and pulled the strap up onto his shoulder. An assault rifle was in easy reach. He armed the car alarm and the engine kill switch and handed the remote to Carrie, who put it in her shoulder bag. Then they took the stairs down to ground level and walked out to the Escalade on the street.

"Time to stir things up," he said.

"What have you got in mind?"

"Let's give Robin a call."

Carrie got out a burner phone, input Robin's number, and put the phone on speaker.

"Hello."

"Hey, Robin. It's Carrie. I've got you on speaker with Philip."

"Cops must be loving you."

"We're doing all right," Carrie said.

"Heard about yesterday's blood bath out a Stafford Circle. Anderson's crew fighting it out with the sex traffickers. How did you manage to make that happen?"

"How do you know it was Anderson's crew?"

"I'm an investigative reporter, remember? Scared working girls were washing up everywhere."

Philip came on the line. "Any of the traffickers escape?"

"I don't think so. And three of the drug crew died at the scene. So why did you do it?"

"Sounds like a good time to leave town."

"You tell me. Are you all done here?"

"Did you know Anderson is using his body shop as a stash house? Maybe your boyfriend would appreciate a tip?"

"Why are you trying to jam up Anderson? What's in it for you?"

"Just providing a public service."

"I heard an interesting story."

"Is that right?"

"I heard that Pollock hired you to kill me, but it was a scam. So when Anderson found out, he sent someone after you. And that's why you're here raining on his parade."

"I bet you hear a lot of crazy stories in your line of work."

Philip glanced at Carrie. She ended the call.

"She's getting close," Carrie said.

"Too close," Philip replied. "I hope the police raid the body shop today."

Carrie put her phone back into her shoulder bag. "You want to set our second car now or have supper first."

"It's the last piece of the puzzle that we have control of, so let's get it done first. It won't take long. We can just pick up something nondescript from a parking lot. Park it on the street near the beltway."

"How about something from the employee parking lot at the twenty-four-hour grocery?"

"Whatever you want."

ROBIN FOUND a parking spot on the street half a block down from Sammy's Pizzaria. Marcos's Dodge was parked in front of the building, but he was still waiting at the hostess stand. "Hey, honey," she said. She slipped her hand in his.

He kissed her. "Long day?"

"Getting longer. Guess who just called me?"

"Philip and Carrie?"

She nodded.

Their waitress, a young, dark-haired woman wearing a white apron over tight jeans and a pink T-shirt, took them to their booth and left them with menus.

"So spill," Marcos said.

"They wanted me to tell you that Anderson is using his body shop as a stash house."

"Probably. But suspicion won't get me a search warrant. We've never been able to get one of his guys to turn on him."

"And I think they got Anderson to go after the sex traffickers."

"They say that?"

"They were cagy, but they didn't deny it."

Their waitress came back and took their order.

Marcos continued. "Well, we've got them as the shooters from the Volvo-Explorer T-bone."

"How so?"

"One of the women from Stafford Circle ID'd the dead guys, said her boss sent them after Philip and Carrie."

"You starting to believe Pollock's story now?"

"I'm starting to believe I could stop these shootouts if I could get my hands on those two. You still don't have any idea where they're staying?"

She shook her head.

"But they're calling you?"

"Yeah. Their phone number keeps changing. I've got a new one now. Maybe it will help." She went into the recent calls on her smartphone and then handed him the phone. "The top number."

He wrote it down. "We'll see what the techs can do with it."

"You'll want to move fast. I don't think they're going to be here much longer."

MEANWHILE, Anderson was on the phone with Kenny. "You found the scammers?"

"Definitely. Night desk clerk at the Holiday Inn Express identified them. They haven't checked out. I've got two guys watching for them."

"Call me when they show."

11

CLEANING UP

Later, after supper, when Philip drove into the parking lot of the Holiday Inn Express, Carrie noticed a white Honda Accord with two men in it watching the front of the motel.

"Those two belong to Anderson," Carrie said.

"Let's make sure they see us."

They walked in through the front doors, Philip carrying their gear bag, and took the elevator up to their room. "How much time do you think we have?" Carrie asked.

"Twenty minutes? Thirty minutes? We'll be fine."

They put on street clothes, sunglasses, and hats over their tactical gear. Carrie had her Glock in her shoulder bag. Philip had his .38 in his ankle holster and his Glock in a holster under his jacket. The AR-15 rifles were in the gear bag.

"You ready?" Carrie asked.

"Just a second."

Philip input the code on the room safe, took out the bag of OxyContin they'd taken from Pollock's office, holding it with two fingers from one corner, and dropped it in the gear bag.

"You think we're going to need that?" Carrie asked.

"Might come in handy."

They left their room, checking the hall to be sure they weren't being watched, and took the stairs at the far end down to the outdoor exit to the swimming pool. Night was falling. The lights around the swimming pool were on. Several children, goggles and inflated toys, were in the water, while their parents sat on the loungers drinking beer. Carrie and Philip nodded as they strolled by and out the gate surrounding the pool.

They could see that the two guys were still sitting in the Honda. They walked around the outside of the parking lot, down the adjacent sidewalk and stopped behind a minivan where they could sneak a good view of the front of the Holiday Inn Express. After a few minutes, a gray Chevy Tahoe pulled up beside the Honda. Four men, including Anderson, got out of the Tahoe. The two men from the Honda joined them. Philip and Carrie slipped down behind them, moving in the shadows among the cars. Just as Anderson's men were starting to fan out, Philip and Carrie positioned themselves behind a nearby Ford Explorer and opened fire with the AR-15s.

Two men fell before they could turn and lift their pistols. Philip and Carrie ducked behind the Explorer and separated, Carrie moving to the left and popping up over the hood of a Nissan, while Philip moved to the right, dropped down on one knee, and fired from around the bumper of a Toyota truck. They caught another man in the crossfire. Anderson and the other two men were scrambling through the parked vehicles, trying to get out of the crossfire and create their own. Philip rolled under the truck and fired at the legs he could see moving a couple of cars over, but they scampered away. Carrie kept the pressure on from behind the Nissan, firing at anyone who popped up between cars, the car's engine protecting her body. As Philip was running between cars, Anderson and both of his men poured fire on Carrie. She ducked down behind the wheel, bullets zinging just above her head. When the firing stopped, she peeked out. Anderson and his men were climbing into the Tahoe.

Philip ran toward her from between a Ford and a Toyota. "You okay?"

"I'm good."

The Tahoe screeched out of the parking lot.

"Let's go."

They ran for the Escalade, jumped in and started off after the Tahoe. "They went right," Carrie said.

Philip careened out of the parking lot, bouncing over the curb. They saw the Tahoe turn right into a residential neighborhood two blocks ahead. Sirens were wailing behind them. When Philip made the turn, they could see the Tahoe under a streetlight in the distance. They had to catch up, deal with them on the road while they were at their most vulnerable.

"Can you catch them?" Carrie asked.

"Are you ready?" he replied.

She pushed a fresh magazine into her assault rifle. "Get me close enough. I'll slow them down."

He pushed the gas pedal down to the floor. The Escalade jumped forward. They were starting to close in. Carrie lowered her window. Wind swirled around the cabin. She hung her jacket over the door to cushion her arm and swung the rife out into position. The Tahoe took another right.

Philip tapped the brake pedal, gripped the steering wheel, and fishtailed around the corner. Carrie rocked back and forth in the window, gripping the rifle with both arms, her teeth clamped together. The Escalade bounced onto the sidewalk. Philip swerved around a maple tree before he got the Escalade back into the street.

"Jesus," Carrie said.

"I know," Philip replied.

"They lost more ground than us." Carrie got back into position. "Get me there before the next turn."

As soon as the Tahoe was within range, Carrie peppered the back end with bullets, shattering the window and punching holes in the liftback. The Tahoe started easing away. "Faster!" Carrie yelled.

"This is all we've got," Philip replied. He heard Carrie change magazines. He could see the holes punched through the shattered safety glass.

"Keep it steady, baby," Carrie said. She fired a burst into the right rear tire. The Tahoe swerved to the right, brake lights flashing. Philip looked straight ahead, pumping his brakes, keeping control of the Escalade, letting Carrie deal with the Tahoe. She fired a burst through the driver's side window as they flew by. He heard a crash. When he got the Escalade stopped, he looked out the back window. The Tahoe was smashed into a massive oak. No one was getting out. He backed up to the wreck. He and Carrie got out, scurried over to the Tahoe with their rifles in their hands, and looked inside. Anderson and both his guys were mangled and bleeding. Philip shot all three of them.

They glanced around. No one was on the street. None of the outdoor lights of the nearby houses had come on, but there had to be people peeking from behind their curtains. Too much noise. Someone must have already called 911. Philip got the bag of OxyContin from the gear bag and tossed it onto Anderson. "Let's go."

They sped up to the first corner, turned left, and then drove at the speed limit, occasionally making a turn, but always moving toward the beltway entrance ramp west of Mason Avenue. When they were about eight blocks away, they heard the distant wail of a firetruck rolling through an intersection.

"EMTs," Carrie said.

"We're making good time."

On Mason Avenue, in a quiet neighborhood of fenced-in yards and well-kept-up Cape Cod houses, Philip pull up beside a tan Camry they'd parked there earlier. Carrie put on fresh gloves and took the tablet to bypass the car's computer. Philip drove up to the end of the block. Carrie got into the Camry and got it started, no fuss, no muss. She followed Philip to an out-of-business Kmart. He parked the Escalade in the middle of the parking lot. She popped the trunk latch on the Camry and got out. Philip carried their gear back to the Camry, dropped it in the trunk, and took out a five gallon can of gas.

"Just be a minute," he said.

He lugged the gas can back to the Escalade, emptied it over the front and back seats, and tossed the empty can into the back. The fumes were thick inside the vehicle. He stepped back, twisted a section of newspaper into a torch and lit it. Carrie got into the Camry and started it. Philip tossed the torch into the Escalade and jogged back to the Camry. Flames were dancing across the seats as they drove away.

"Now we're just got to pick up the Highlander and put the Camry back."

"Sure you want to take the extra time?"

"Cops will never find it if it's back where it belongs."

DETECTIVES Marcos and Bledsoe got out of their Dodge at the crime scene on McKinley Drive. The street was blocked from both sides and police tape marked off the area where the shell casings had fallen around the smashed Chevy Tahoe. The EMTs had found three men dead at the scene, broken up from the crash and shot for good measure. They'd been transported after CSI had taken their pictures. Detective Lewis stood by the Tahoe, talking to Jerry Gordon.

"Hey, Troy, Jerry," Marcos said.

Bledsoe whistled. "So this is where the shootout at the Holiday Inn Express ended up. What a mess."

"Six dead," Lewis replied. "Three here and three at the motel."

"Citizens or players?"

"They all look like players."

"Anybody we know?" Marcos asked.

"Not at the Holiday Inn," Gordon said. "The three here are pretty messed up, but one of them looks a lot like Dylan Anderson."

Lewis nodded. "The Tahoe's registered to Samuel Hillerman, but he was home in bed. The SUV was supposed to be at A-Okay Autobody. So it probably is Anderson. What brings you two out?"

"Chasing leads on our drug case," Bledsoe said.

"I hear you got a theory that ties all these murder cases together."

"It's looking that way," Marcos said. "Every one of these shootouts in the last week involves a man and a woman who always manage to get away. Mike's case, your other case, and all the cases involving Anderson's crew."

"Description?" Lewis asked.

"The Budget Inn is the only place they were caught wearing street clothes," Marcos replied.

"Well then we're screwed, because the surveillance video is crap and the witness descriptions are so vague they're useless."

"What about the Toyota Highlander?" Marcos asked.

"Without the plate number, we've got nothing."

Bledsoe turned to Gordon. "And there's no evidence here that's of any use?"

"We'll be processing the Holiday Inn and this one first thing in the morning," Gordon said. "Maybe something will turn up."

"We'll give you a call," Bledsoe said.

Marcos turned to Lewis, "Good luck, Troy."

"I won't need any luck if your theory's correct. The cases will be consolidated, and I'll be off the hook." Lewis waved at the tow truck to pick up the Tahoe for transport to the police impound lot.

Marcos and Bledsoe walked away. "That phone number you got from Robin is our best bet," Bledsoe said.

Marcos shook his head. "We'll see. Techs said tomorrow or the next day to trace the carrier. After that we need a warrant."

THE NEXT MORNING, Marcos and Bledsoe went to see Jerry Gordon down in the police lab. Anderson had been positively identified via fingerprints from the TSA PreCheck database. "What did he die of?" Marcos asked.

"Preliminary? The crash killed him," Gordon said.

"What did he have on him?"

"The usual. Keys, wallet, phone. There were guns found in the car, but we haven't processed them for fingerprints yet. And we found a bag of OxyContin in the floor of the Tahoe."

Bledsoe snorted. "A bag of Oxy?"

Gordon nodded. "The same stuff we've been finding everywhere."

"What about the rest of his crew?"

"They all had records. I'll send you the full file before five o'clock."

"What about the surveillance camera from the Holiday Inn Express?"

"It was in exactly the right place. Anderson and his guys were banging away like they were in Bagdad."

"Any film of the other crew?" Marcos asked.

"Man and a woman. Tactical gear and ski masks."

"Like the Volvo-Explorer T-bone and the strip mall hit?"

"You got it. Not definitive, but that's who it looks like. Footage from earlier in the day showed a couple getting in and out of a Toyota Highlander who look similar to the couple from the Budget Inn. We can't make out their faces, but we got four plate numbers."

"They weren't driving the Highlander when they took off after the Tahoe?"

"No, that was an Escalade. Uniforms found it on fire at the old Kmart. Total loss."

"Thanks, Jerry," Marcos said. "Keep us up to speed."

"You bet."

Marcos and Bledsoe walked back down the hall to the elevator. "We aren't any closer to our mystery couple," Marcos said, "but between the Oxy and the surveillance footage from the Holiday Inn parking lot, I bet we can get an expedited search warrant for A-Okay Autobody."

"You think?" Bledsoe said. "This case just blew up big time. And we need to have patrol cars start checking motels for a Highlander with those plate numbers."

When they pulled up to A-Okay Autobody at 10:00 a.m., the gate was padlocked. Several autobody technicians were standing in a group on the side of the road, their cars parked along the right of way.

Marcos showed his badge. "Cornwell PD. Who's in charge?"

"The boss went to get a key," one man said.

Marcos took Anderson's keys out of his pocket, found the right one, and opened the padlock. "We have a search warrant. You guys need to wait out here until we're through."

Marcos and Bledsoe drove down to the building. Marcos found the office key and opened the door. In the reception area, a sofa was shoved back against the windows, a coffee table flipped over on the cushions. Two chairs were stacked beside it. Carpet tack strips ran around the perimeter of what appeared to be a freshly washed concrete floor. "Looks like they took up the carpeting," Marcos said.

"Didn't Anderson say this office was under construction?" Bledsoe asked.

"That was the story."

They moved from the reception area down into the hallway: accounting department, what appeared to be Anderson's office, and a locked storeroom.

"Another new door," Marcos said. He unlocked the storeroom. Shelves of supplies and a six-foot by three-foot safe. "We need a safe specialist."

Bledsoe made the call. "He'll be a half hour."

They went back outside the offices to wait. A few minutes later, an older man wearing technician's coveralls walked down from the gate. "What's going on?"

"You the manager?" Marcos asked.

He nodded.

Marcos showed his badge again. "Cornwell PD. We have a search warrant."

"I don't know anything about what to do about that," the manager said.

"You don't do anything," Bledsoe replied. "You can watch if you like, but you stay out of the way until we're done."

"Did you call Mr. Anderson?"

"We don't have to," Bledsoe said.

"Then I guess I better watch." He stood off to one side.

Forty minutes later, the safe specialist, a bearlike man wearing round glasses and a golf shirt with Dependable Vault and Safes embroidered on the chest, parked his work van next to Marcos's Dodge and wheeled a toolbox out of the back. "You guys called?"

Marcos and Bledsoe nodded.

"I need to see the warrant."

Marcos handed it to him. He read it and took a photo with his phone. "Thanks. Just making sure all the paperwork is right. Where's the safe?"

They led him back through the offices to the storage room, the manager trailing behind them. "Keep your hands in your pockets."

"Okay," the manager said.

The safe specialist set his toolbox next to the safe and then examined the serial numbers etched into the side. "Your lucky day, guys. This is one of ours. Let me call the office for the override code."

A few minutes later he pulled open the door. The middle and lower shelf were stacked with gallon-size plastic bags. Marcos slipped on a throwaway glove, pulled a bag out and looked at the pills through the plastic. "OxyContin."

"I've just got one question," Bledsoe said. "Where's the money?"

Marcos turned to the safe specialist and the manager. "You two are witnesses. The safe was locked. These bags of drugs are all we found. We'll take your statements after CSI gets here."

Marcos got out his smartphone and called dispatch to alert Jerry Gordon. Then he walked out into the parking lot and called Robin.

"What's up?"

"I'm at A-Okay Autobody. You know Anderson was killed last night?"

"Yes."

"We just found a load of drugs in his safe at the shop."

"I'm on my way."

WHEN ROBIN ARRIVED at A-Okay Autobody, she drove past the autobody techs hanging around the gate and parked next to the CSI van. Joel was waiting for her by the door to the offices. "How good is it?" she asked.

"It's the jackpot," he said. "Put this on." He handed her a throw-away glove to put on her free hand. "And don't touch anything. You don't want to smear any fingerprints."

He led the way to the storeroom. Bledsoe, the safe specialist, and the shop manager were watching Gordon and two techs photograph the interior of the safe and box up the gallon bags of pills for processing in the lab. "Hey, Steve, hey, Jerry," she said to Bledsoe and Gordon.

Bledsoe shook his finger at Marcos. "You had to, didn't you?"

Marcos shrugged. "You want credit, don't you?"

Gordon glanced over his shoulder. "Robin, somehow I'm not surprised you're here."

"So the pills were all you found?" Robin asked. "No cash?"

"Not a dime," Bledsoe replied.

"When was the last time the drug task force found a haul like this?"

"I don't know," Marcos replied.

"I'd have to check the records," Gordon said.

"So you'd call this unusual?" she continued.

"It's amazing," Gordon replied. "Assuming the pills are genuine."

"Do they look like the pills that came from Pollock's office?"

He shrugged.

"Is that a yes or a maybe?"

"It's a maybe until the analysis comes back."

"I'll be calling you for your comments later." She turned back to Marcos and Bledsoe. "Can I interview the witnesses?"

"Sure," Marcos said. "We're done with them."

After Robin finished talking with the shop manager and the safe specialist, she took pictures of the open safe, the storage room, the reception area, and the front of the building.

Marcos walked her out to her car. "Happy now?"

"Ecstatic."

"We're still looking for Philip and Carrie."

"If I hear from them, you'll be the first to know."

"We going out to dinner to celebrate?"

She gave him a quick kiss. “Call me later.”

Robin turned right out of the parking lot, taking the shortest route downtown to the *Herald* offices. OxyContin distribution leading from Pollock back to Anderson. A trail of murder and attempted murder. Had this story really broken open because Pollock botched the hiring of a hit man and instead paid his money to a murder-for-hire scam? Was that the original domino? Joel shot Peanut Frazier while he was trying to kill her. But all the others? Philip and Carrie came to town looking for payback. They set Anderson’s crew on the sex traffickers—they’d admitted as much. But was that because of Gypsy or just to narrow their odds? And Anderson’s guys? Travis Smith murdered at the strip mall. Jim Lee found at a bus stop. The shootout at the Holiday Inn Express. The wrecked Tahoe. Had Philip and Carrie found a way to kill all of them? And where was the money that should have been in the safe? Pollock was lucky to still be alive. She got out her phone.

“Carrie, I’m surprised you answered.”

“Where are you?” Carrie asked.

“Driving back from A-Okay Autobody.”

“I take it congratulations are in order.”

“Did you guys take care of Anderson?”

Philip came on the line. “Robin, you need to take a win when you’ve got a win. Write your big story. Leave us out of it.”

“That might be hard to do.”

“Without making yourself look like a gullible fool or an accessory to murder? Cooperating with criminals to aid their criminal enterprise? You’ll have a hell of a time proving you didn’t know what we planned to do. Anonymous tips and reporter’s intuition make for a much better story.”

“I just want to know one thing.”

“You never stop, do you?”

“Why did you get involved with Gypsy? She didn’t have anything to do with your plans. And why did you help me? You could have just followed Frazier. You would have found Anderson soon enough.”

Philip chuckled. “Some things you’re just going to have to figure out for yourself."

He ended the call. Robin shook her head. He was right. All the cops had was surveillance footage and eyewitness testimony of tactical-clad killers. Nothing to tie them to any crime. But the parts she could prove still made a great story. And Pollock was still a live wire.

PHILIP AND CARRIE lay together in bed in a room at the Hilton Garden Inn in Danville, Illinois. "What time is it?" Philip asked.

Carrie looked at the face of the burner phone. "Eleven thirty."

"Robin is relentless. Can't have her calling anymore."

Carrie pulled the chip from the phone, broke it between her fingers, and set it on the night table. "We needed to get up anyway."

Philip sat up out of bed. "You're right. We've dropped too many bodies and stole too many cars back in Cornwell. Plus Robin knows the Highlander. We need to switch cars, dump any clothes with gunpower residue on them, and get farther down the road before we slow down."

"You want me to call Billy to pick up the heavy gear?" she asked.

"You can do that in the car. Let's get out of here, go through a MacDonald's drive-through and put some more miles between us and Cornwell."

AFTER THEY FINISHED at A-Okay Autobody, Marcos and Bledsoe took their time driving back to the police station to start in on the paperwork.

"Big case for us," Bledsoe said.

"Yes, indeed."

"A drug haul and Anderson out of the picture. Pollock's pill mill shut down."

"A big win for the drug task force, that's for sure. If we had a lead on the mystery couple, we'd be batting one thousand," Marcos said.

"Never going to find them with just four license plate numbers."

"If they're even driving the same car."

"What about the telephone number?"

"I'm not holding out any hope."

"What do you want to do about consolidating the murder cases?" Bledsoe asked. "Mike and Troy aren't going to let up about it."

"Do you want to get stuck with those cases? A man and woman—no real descriptions—get into a war with Anderson and a gang of sex traffickers. Property damage, but no citizens killed. Illegal drug trade disrupted."

"A lot of bodies."

"All criminals. Unless that mystery couple decides to take over the drug trade, they're off our radar," Marcos said.

"Mike and Troy aren't going to like it."

"Look, we got stuck with the OD'd prostitute."

"Probable misadventure."

"And Travis Smith, Jim Lee, and the Stafford house shootout," Marcos continued.

"Fair enough. But we get credit for the drug bust at the body shop."

"Because we did the police work. And Mike doesn't have anything to complain about. He only got the two sex traffickers at the T-bone. And they've got nothing to do with the drug task force."

"Yeah, but the Holiday Inn Express and the Tahoe killings led directly to the A-Okay search warrant."

"So we'll take that one off Troy's hands. But the Budget Inn? There's no proof Anderson was anywhere near that."

"They may go to the captain with the mystery couple theory."

"Let them try. We're going to have a hell of a time as it is working the five cases we've consolidated in the Anderson file. Mike and Troy caught a couple of tough cases—that's just how it worked out—and they're going to have to do the best they can. You're not going to make me feel sorry for either of them."

THE NEXT MORNING, Robin's story about the A-Okay Autobody stash house ran on the front page of the *Cornwell Herald*. It was the first of a planned series of stories on the connections among overprescribing of pain medication, Pollock's pill mill, Anderson's illegal drug trafficking, and overdose deaths. With Anderson dead and Pollock under arrest, many people, including many of Pollock's patients, were clamoring to tell their stories on the record.

Robin's landline phone in the newsroom rang, but she didn't answer it. The quality of the leads was dropping by the hour as attention-seekers, hoping to get their name in the paper, left vague messages on her voice mail. She was curious, though, if Pollock was ready to talk. She gave him another call.

"Dr. Pollock? Robin Simons from the *Herald*."

"What can I do for you?"

"Are you ready to make a statement on the record?"

"Sorry. I'm afraid I can't say anything without consulting my lawyer."

"Is there anything you'd like to tell me on background?"

"Off the record?"

"Completely."

"Anderson threatened my family. If I didn't sell his pills, his men were going to kill us."

"What about all the money you made? What about all that spin about helping patients get their pain medication?"

"I never would have done any of it if I hadn't been afraid for my life."

"That's your story now?"

"It's the truth. Ask my employees. They'll back me up."

"I might just do that."

"Look, I'm one of the victims here. My wife's filed for divorce. My patients are leaving my practice. I won't be able to pay my legal fees in another month."

"Call me when you're ready to talk on the record."

THAT AFTERNOON, in the parking lot of the Shriner's Park, Kenny sat in his Avalon with the air-conditioning running. Elementary-age children played on the swings and the jungle gym, their parents sitting on the nearby benches. Further away, a middle school age club soccer team was practicing drills. Manuel, his hood up on his sweatshirt, came down into the parking lot from the woods to the right of the playground and tapped his fist against the passenger's side window before he got into the car.

"Hey, Kenny."

Kenny grinned. "So you weren't at the shootout."

"Dylan made me stay back at the body shop to protect the stash."

"Lucky you."

Manuel shrugged. "You weren't there, either."

"No, I wasn't. And I don't feel bad about it. Dylan lost his edge. Thought he was smarter than everybody else. Rushed into an ambush."

"I hear you."

"Have you seen any of the other guys?"

"Just Peanut's buddy, Toots."

"You want to stay away from him. Cops will be watching Peanut's place."

"What're you going to do?"

"I'm going to reach out to Dylan's connection. Get as many of our spots back up and running as possible."

"You're taking over?"

"That's right. You ready to step up?"

"Tell me what to do."

LATER THAT EVENING, Philip and Carrie stopped at a Quality Inn on the interstate. They'd bought a Cadillac at a used-car dealer and dumped the Highlander into a lake in a state park. An empty duffel bag sat on the bed closest to the motel room door, a cascade of rubber-banded money beside it.

"So what's the final count?" Philip opened the calculator on his smartphone.

Carrie glanced down at the bank statement on her smartphone. "We made $25,000 from the original con."

"Shame that's blown," Philip said. "I was hoping that scam would last for six months at least."

She picked up two bundles. "The seventy thousand from Anderson's home safe." Then she counted through the bundles still lying on the bed. "Three thousand from Pollock, another four thousand and change from the courier, and"—she pushed her hands through the remaining piles—"the one hundred seventy-two thousand from the body shop."

Philip looked up from the calculator. "That's $274,000 total. That's amazing money." He did a division. "Three-way split means $91,333 for Merlin's family, and $182,667 for us. We'll eat the expenses."

"Ninety-one thousand will carry them through the year. Give his wife time to catch her breath and figure out what she's going to do."

"He deserved that much."

"And we cleared $140,000 easy after paying for the cars and gear. That's real vacation money, even if there was too much gunplay," Carrie said.

"The gunplay wasn't in the scam, it was in the payback. But I take your point."

"That's where most of the money was, too."

"We're still not completely in the clear, though. We need fresh IDs."

"Kansas City or Omaha?"

"Jonesy retired, so we'll have to go to Kansas City," Philip replied.

"Haven't been there in a long time. It's a fun city."

"They've got great barbeque down there."

"Maybe we can take in some baseball or hear some jazz," Carrie said.

"After we set up our new IDs, we can do whatever you want."

Carrie started stacking the bundles of money back into the duffel bag. "Where do you want to go on vacation?"

Philip smiled. "That's a tough decision. Let's talk about it tomorrow on the drive down to Missouri."

A NOTE FROM THE AUTHOR

Thanks for reading *The Dark Web Scam*. If you enjoyed it, please post a short review on a review site of your choice. A few words will do. Honest reviews are the number one way I attract new readers.

Thanks so much.

I'd love to hear from you. You can reach me at my website: https://michaelpking.org

The Travelers

The Double Cross: A Travelers Prequel
The Traveling Man: Book One
The Computer Heist: Book Two
The Blackmail Photos: Book Three
The Freeport Robbery: Book Four
The Kidnap Victim: Book Five
The Murder Run: Book Six
The Casino Switcheroo: Book Seven
Thicker Than Thieves: Book Eight
The Dark Web Scam: Book Nine

www.ingramcontent.com/pod-product-compliance
Lightning Source LLC
LaVergne TN
LVHW041928090826
845145LV00017B/2294

9781952711022